## Praise for John Kennedy Toole and *The Neon Bible*

"A powerful novel that belongs on the shelf with the works of Flannery O'Connor, Carson McCullers, and Eudora Welty. It is a moving evocation of the small-town South in the mid-twentieth century, and it is an expertly crafted tale of an adolescent boy finding the courage to make the decisions to change his life."  —William McKeen, *Orlando Sentinel*

"Shockingly mature . . . Even at sixteen, Toole knew that the way to write about complex emotions is to express them simply."  —Kerry Luft, *Chicago Tribune*

"Heartfelt emotion, communicated in clean direct prose . . . a remarkable achievement."
—Michiko Kakutani, *The New York Times*

"About as good as juvenilia can get—and eloquent testimony to the magnitude of our loss."  —*Kirkus Reviews*

"There is a touch of genius about Toole and what he has created."  —*Publishers Weekly,* on *A Confederacy of Dunces*

"A masterwork."
—*New York Times Book Review,* on *A Confederacy of Dunces*

"The dialogue is superbly mad. You simply sweep along, unbelievably entranced."
—*Boston Globe,* on *A Confederacy of Dunces*

"An astonishingly original and assured comic spree."
—*New York,* on *A Confederacy of Dunces*

# The
# Neon Bible

# The
# Neon Bible

## JOHN KENNEDY TOOLE

Grove Press
*New York*

*Published simultaneously in Canada*
*Printed in the United States of America*

First Grove Atlantic edition: May 1989

Library of Congress Catalog Card Number 88-26074

ISBN 978-0-8021-3207-9
eISBN 978-0-8021-9732-0

Grove Press
an imprint of Grove Atlantic
154 West 14th Street
New York, NY 10011

Distributed by Publishers Group West

groveatlantic.com

19 20 21 22   25 24 23 22 21 20 19

# The
# Neon Bible

# One

This is the first time I've been on a train. I've sat in this seat here for about two or three hours now. I can't see what's passing by. It's dark now, but when the train left, the sun was just beginning to set, and I could see the red and brown leaves and the tanning grass all along the hillside.

I feel a little better the further the train gets from the house. The tingling that has been running up and down the inside of my legs is stopping, and my feet feel like they're really there now, and not like two cold things that don't really belong to the rest of my body. I'm not as scared anymore.

There's a colored fellow coming through between the seats. He's snapped off every one of the lights over the seats. There's just a tiny red one glowing at the end of the coach, and I'm sorry it isn't bright here anymore by my seat, because I start to think too much in the dark about what's back in the house. They must have turned the heat off too. It's cold in here. I wish I had a blanket to throw over my knees and something to put over this seat so the plush wouldn't scratch the back of my neck.

If it was day outside, I could see where I was. I've never been this far from home in my life. We must be almost two hundred miles away now. With nothing to see, you have to listen to the click-click-click of the train. Sometimes I hear the whistle sounding far ahead. I've heard it plenty times, but I never thought I'd be riding with it. And I don't mind the clicking. It sounds like the rain on a tin roof at night when it's quiet and still and the only thing you can hear is the rain and the thunder.

But I had a train of my own. It was a toy one I got for Christmas when I was three. That was when Poppa was working at the factory and we lived in the little white house in town that had a real roof you could sleep under when it rained, and not a tin one like the place on the hill had that leaked through the nail holes too.

People came to see us that Christmas. We always had some people in the house, coming in blowing and rubbing their hands together and shaking out their coats like it was snowing outside. But there was no snow. Not that year. But they were nice, and brought me things. I remember the preacher gave me a book of Bible stories. But that was most likely because my mother and father were paying church members then, with their names on the rolls and both of them in the Adult Study Class that met every Sunday at nine and Wednesday night at seven for a social. I was in the Pre-School Play section, but we never played like the name said.

We had to listen to stories some old woman read to us out of a grownup book that we didn't understand.

Mother was very hospitable that year I got the train. Everybody got some of her fruitcake that she was proud of. She said it was from an old family recipe, but I found out later she got the cake through a mail order from some company in Wisconsin called the Olde English Baking Company, Limited. I found that out when I learned to read and saw it in the mail a few Christmases later when we didn't have any people over and we had to eat it ourselves. No one ever knew, though, that she didn't make it, except me and Mother and maybe the man at the post office, but he was a deaf mute and couldn't tell anybody.

I don't remember any children my age coming around that Christmas. As a matter of fact, there weren't any children my age living around us at all. After Christmas was over, I stayed in the house and played with my train. It was too cold outside, and about January it began to snow. Heavy snows that year, although everyone thought they'd never come.

It was that spring that Mother's Aunt Mae came to live with us. She was heavy but not fat, and about sixty, and came from out of state somewhere where they had nightclubs. I asked Mother why her hair wasn't shiny and yellow like Aunt Mae's, and she said some people were just lucky, and I felt sorry for her.

Next to the train, I remember Aunt Mae most. She smelled so strong of perfume that sometimes you couldn't get near her without your nose stinging and having a hard time getting air. I never saw anybody with hair and clothes like that, and I sat and just looked at her sometimes.

When I was four Mother gave a party for some of the wives of the factory workers, and Aunt Mae came into the living room in the middle of the party wearing a dress that showed almost all her front, except for the nipples, which I knew you never could show. The party ended soon after that, and as I was sitting on the porch, I heard the women talking to each other as they left. And they were calling Aunt Mae all sorts of names like I had never heard before and really didn't know the meaning of until I was almost ten years old.

"You had no right to dress that way," Mother told her later when they were sitting in the kitchen. "You've deliberately hurt me and all of Frank's friends. If I knew you were going to act this way, I would never have let you come to live with us."

Aunt Mae ran her finger over the button of the robe Mother had put on her. "But Sarah, I didn't know they'd take on that way. Why, I've worn that gown before audiences from Charleston to New Orleans. I forgot to show you my clippings, didn't I? The notices, the notices! They were superb, particularly about that gown."

"Look, dear"—Mother was pouring some of the special sherry in Aunt Mae's glass to humor her—"on the stage that gown may have been quite successful, but you don't know what it's like to live in a small town like this. If Frank hears about things like that, he won't let you stay here. Now, don't ever do that to me again."

The sherry made Aunt Mae quiet, but I knew that she hadn't paid any attention to what Mother had said. It surprised me, though, to hear that Aunt Mae had been "on the stage." I had seen the stage at the Town Hall, but the only things I had seen there were men making speeches, and I wondered just what Aunt Mae had done "on the stage." I couldn't see her as a speechmaker, so one day I asked her what she had done, and she pulled a big black scrapbook out of her trunk and showed it to me.

On the first page there was a picture from a newspaper of a slender young girl with black hair and a feather in it. She looked cross-eyed to me, but Aunt Mae said that was only where the paper had touched up the picture wrong. She read me what it said under the picture: "Mae Morgan, popular singer at the Rivoli." Then she said that the picture was a picture of her, and I said it couldn't be because she didn't have black hair, and besides, her name was Gebler, not Morgan. But she told me that both of these had been changed for "theatrical purposes," so we turned the page. The rest of the book was the same, except that in every picture Aunt Mae got fatter, and near the middle of it, her hair turned blonde. Toward the end there were fewer pictures, and they were so small that the only way I could tell it was Aunt Mae was by her hair.

Although the book didn't interest me, it made me like Aunt Mae more, and somehow it made her seem more important to me. I would sit near her at dinner and listen to everything she said, and one day Poppa began to ask me everything Aunt Mae said to me when we were together, and kept on asking me every day after that. I told him how Aunt Mae told me about the count who used to kiss her hand and always ask her to marry him and go to live with him in Europe. And about the time some man drank wine out of one of her slippers. And I told Poppa that he must've been drunk. And all the time Poppa just said uh-huh, uh-huh.

And at night I'd hear him and Mother arguing in their room.

But until I began school, I still saw a lot of Aunt Mae. She didn't go to church on Sunday with us, but in the afternoon she would take me walking down Main Street, and we'd look at all the window displays, and even though she was old enough to be my grandmother, men would turn and look at her, and wink too. I saw our butcher do that one Sunday, and I knew he had children because I had seen a little girl playing in his store. I never had a chance to see what Aunt Mae was doing because she had a feather boa that hid her face from me. But I think she winked back at the men. She wore her skirts to her knees, too, and I remember hearing women talk about it.

We walked up and down Main Street all afternoon until it got dark, but never through the park or into the hills where I really wanted to go. I was always so happy when the displays in the windows were changed, because I got tired of seeing the same pictures week after week. Aunt Mae stopped us on the busiest corner, and we saw the display there so often that it almost crowded the train out of my dreams. Once I asked Aunt Mae if she ever got tired of seeing that same picture of the man advertising the razor blades, but she told me to just keep on looking at it and maybe it would teach me how to shave for when I was older. One day, after the display had been taken out of the window of that store, I went into Aunt Mae's room to get her glasses for her, and there was that picture of the man in the undershirt with the razor blade tacked up in her closet. For some reason or other, I never asked her just how or why it was there.

Aunt Mae was good to me, though. She bought me little

toys and taught me how to play games and would take me to the movies on Saturdays. After we had seen Jean Harlow a few times, I began to notice that Aunt Mae was talking through her nose and wearing her hair pulled behind her ears and hanging on her shoulders. She stuck her stomach out, too, when she walked.

Sometimes she would grab me and hug me close right between her bosom so that I was almost smothered. Then she would kiss me with her big mouth and leave lipstick marks all over me. And when I sat in her lap, she told me stories about her days on the stage, and her boyfriends, and the presents she got. She was my only playmate, and we got along all the time. We'd go out walking, with her so funny with her buttocks all sucked in and her stomach stuck out like a pregnant Jean Harlow, and me always so small and sick-looking. No one who didn't know us would think we were in any way related.

Mother was glad to see that we were such good friends. She always had more time to work because Aunt Mae and I were playing together. Aunt Mae kidded, too. She told me that when I got older, I could be her boyfriend. And when I took it seriously, she laughed and laughed. And then I laughed too, because I had never been kidded before and didn't know how.

The town then was a little quieter than it is now, because the war made it a little larger. And if it was quieter than it is now, you can imagine just how quiet it must have been. Aunt Mae was so different from everybody else that she just naturally attracted attention. When she first moved in with us, I remember everyone asked Mother what kind of a relation she was. Although she was so well known, she was never invited anywhere, and the women never got friendly with her. The men were always nice, though, but used to laugh about her when she wasn't around. It made me feel bad when they did, because there wasn't a man in town Aunt Mae didn't like.

When he wasn't mad at the way she was dressing or walking, Poppa laughed at her too. Mother told him that Aunt Mae was really very pitiful and that he shouldn't laugh at her. And that made me wonder. Aunt Mae wasn't pitiful. At least I didn't think so. And I told Mother what I thought too, and that just made Poppa laugh more. And then I was mad at Poppa and never told him again what Aunt Mae would talk to me about. And then we were mad at each other, and I was sorry I had said anything at all. But I still didn't think Aunt Mae was pitiful.

Aunt Mae said that I was getting paler and paler, so we went out walking every afternoon. Personally I thought I was getting taller and much pinker around the cheeks, but I had nothing to do, so I went with her. We had just seen a movie with Jean Harlow and Franchot Tone, so Aunt Mae put some grease in my hair and put a tie on me and said that I did look something like him.

We began our daily walks, and at first I liked them, but after a while everyone in town came out to see us go by and laughed as we passed. Aunt Mae said that it was just jealousy, but anyway, our walks stopped except for Sunday.

Although I never suspected it, I was getting very well known in town just because I walked out with Aunt Mae. And people began to tell Poppa that his little boy was very famous. That was one of the reasons the walks stopped.

Even though she never spoke to hardly anyone, Aunt Mae

knew all the gossip around town and could even tell Mother things she never knew.

It was about this time that Poppa decided I should go play with other little boys instead of Aunt Mae. I didn't think too much about it because I didn't know what little boys were like. I had only seen boys my age on the street, but I never had a chance to meet them. So I was sent to play with the son of one of Poppa's friends at the factory. Every day when Poppa left for the factory, he would take me to the man's house. When I first met the boy, I didn't know what to say or what to do. He was about six, and a little bit bigger than I was, and his name was Bruce. The first thing he did was grab my cap off my head and throw it into the stream by his house. I didn't know what to do then, so I just began to cry. Poppa laughed at me and told me to fight him back, but I didn't know how. I had a terrible time that day and wanted to be back home with Mother and Aunt Mae. Bruce could do anything. Climb, jump, fight, throw. I followed behind him and tried to do what he did. At lunchtime his mother called us in and gave us some sandwiches and told me that if Bruce did anything to me to just give it back to him. And I nodded, and said yes, I would. When she turned away, Bruce knocked my milk glass over, and his mother turned around and thought I did it and slapped me in the face. Bruce laughed, and she told us to go outside and play. That was the first time I had been slapped on the face, and it made me feel terrible. I could hardly do anything after that, so Bruce went to get some of his friends to play. When he left, I vomited my sandwich and milk in the bushes and sat down and began to cry.

"You been crying," Bruce said to me when he returned.

The two friends he had brought with him were about seven and looked big to me.

"No, I haven't." I got up off the ground and blinked my bloodshot eyes to try to clear the tears up.

"You're a sissy!" One of Bruce's friends had his hand tight on my collar. I felt my throat lump up. I didn't know what that word meant, but from the way he said it, I knew it wasn't anything good. I looked over at Bruce, thinking he might come between me and this boy. He just stood there looking damn satisfied.

Then the first sock came. It was on my head right above my eye, and I began to cry again, only this time harder. They were all on me at once, I thought. I felt myself falling backward, and I landed with them on top of me. My stomach made a sick grinding noise, and I started feeling the vomit climb up into my throat. I was tasting blood on my lips now, and an awful scaredness was creeping from my feet up my legs. I felt the tingling go up till it grabbed me where I really felt it. Then the vomit came, over everything. Me, Bruce, and the other two. They screamed and jumped off me. And I laid there and the sun was hot and there was dust all over me.

When Poppa came to get me in the evening, I was sitting on Bruce's front porch. The dust and blood and vomit were all still on me, and they were caked now. He looked at me for a while, and I didn't say anything to him. He took me by the hand. We had to walk halfway across town to get home. All the time we didn't say one word to each other.

That night is a night I'll never forget. Mother and Aunt Mae cried over me and disinfected me and whatnot, and listened while I told them what had happened, and how

Bruce's mother wouldn't let me in the house but made me wait on the porch all afternoon till Poppa came. I told them that Poppa hadn't talked to me all the way home, and Aunt Mae called him names, but Mother just looked at him in the strangest sad way. He never talked the whole night, but just sat there in the kitchen reading the paper. I'm sure he must've read it over ten times.

I finally got to bed all bandaged up and feeling sore and hurt all over. Mother slept with me, because I heard her say to Aunt Mae that she couldn't sleep with Poppa, not tonight. She asked me was I feeling better, and it felt good to have her near me. It made me forget the sores and my stomach that still felt sick.

After that, I was never as friendly with Poppa as I was before, and he felt the same way about me. I didn't like it at all. Sometimes I wished we could be friends again, but there was something wrong neither of us could change. In a way I tried to blame it on Aunt Mae. At first I thought she had made him not talk to me. But I couldn't blame it on her for long, and no one could ever not trust her.

By this time I was five. I was getting around the age to go to the county school, but Aunt Mae said I could wait another year and strengthen up some. Besides our Sunday walks, she began to play with me outdoors, and I must admit she knew a lot of rough games. When she wasn't feeling well, we'd just sit in the mud and play with my toy cars. Aunt Mae would sit down with her legs crossed on the ground and run one of the cars over the little hill I had made. She was wearing slacks now because she saw Marlene Dietrich wearing them in some magazine. Jean Harlow was dead, and out of respect for her passing, Aunt Mae didn't walk like her anymore.

This made me feel better, anyway. Especially on Sunday afternoons. When we played with the cars, Aunt Mae always took the truck and played the truck driver. She drove carelessly, I thought, and one time rammed her truck into my hand by mistake and made it bleed. Since I doubt if I had much blood in me anyway, it didn't make a mess.

"David," Aunt Mae would say, "you must show more spirit with your car. You go too slow. Now, let me show you how to handle this."

And she'd make her truck go so fast that it would knock up the dust all around us. And that would bury some of my small toys, so that I lost one or two every time we played cars. When we came in in the late afternoon, we were always dirty, and Aunt Mae would have to wash her hair. I sat on a chair by the tub and watched her hang her head over the basin to wash the soap out of her yellow hair. One time she sent me to her closet to get a little bottle for her. She'd rinse the stuff through her hair when she was finished washing it. I took the bottle back and put it on the shelf next to the razor blade man's picture, which was getting pretty yellow around the edges. The shaving cream in the picture, and the undershirt too, were very faded, and there were lipstick marks on his face where they never were before. The marks were so large that I knew they had to be Aunt Mae's.

I was getting bigger, and this was because of the playing outdoors with Aunt Mae. She was getting bigger too. This made her start on a diet, because she said she had to keep her "figure." But I didn't know what she meant, because she never did have anything special in the first place. Her hair was getting longer, and she wore roses in it behind her ears. In the front it was high and combed over a big false piece of cotton. From there it hung down behind her ears and behind the roses and ended on her back in a lot of curls. It attracted so much attention that a lot of the young girls in town began to wear their hair that way. Aunt Mae was very proud of this and mentioned it to Mother all the time. She tried to get Mother to wear her hair that way too, but she never succeeded.

So I felt that things had gone from bad to worse. When we went out on Sundays, Aunt Mae's hair and the slacks got more attention than the Jean Harlow walk had ever done. She told me that maybe she could make some "contacts" now that she had the new style. I didn't know what she meant, but there were more winks at her after that, and she wore her feather boa higher so I couldn't see her face at all.

It was about that time Aunt Mae got her boyfriend. I had seen him around town before, and I think he worked in one of the groceries. He must've been seventy years old. We first met him one day when we were out walking. We were looking in a window display when Aunt Mae whispered that someone was following us. We started off again, and I heard this shuffle-shuffle-hop behind us. I turned around and saw this old man following us. He was looking straight at Aunt Mae's buttocks, which at the time were pretty flabby because she wasn't sucking them in anymore. When he saw that I saw him, he looked away quick and started studying one of the window advertisements. It made me feel funny to know that he was looking at Aunt Mae in that particular place. Next Sunday he stopped and talked to us, and Aunt Mae acted like I had never seen her act before. She acted cute and giggled at everything he said. This won him over, or seemed to anyway, because he began calling on her at night the next week.

At first they just sat in the living room talking and drinking tea. Poppa seemed to like it, because he knew the old man and said he was good for Aunt Mae. I didn't tell Poppa what he had been looking at that day on the street. I didn't tell Aunt Mae either. She seemed to like the old man, and I knew she wouldn't believe me if I told her. I didn't know what he wanted, but I did know that it wasn't nice to look at anyone in that place.

After he had come around about a month, they started sitting on the porch, and I remember hearing Aunt Mae's giggle below me as I went to sleep at night. The next morning she would come down to breakfast late and usually be angry at everything. This went on all during that summer, and the old man, whose name was George, was at the house almost every night. He smelled of Lilac Vegetal, and between him and Aunt Mae I wondered how the two of them could be together without choking each other. I didn't know what they did on the porch. I never thought they could be making love like young people did in the movies. When the nights of Aunt Mae's giggling passed, those two began to be very quiet on the porch. And one morning, before dawn, when Mother was taking me to the bathroom, we passed Aunt Mae's room and she wasn't in there yet. I never asked Aunt Mae why she was still on the porch at three in the morning, but I remember wanting to.

During this time I saw very little of Aunt Mae. After she came to breakfast, she would play with me in a halfhearted way for a while, and then return to her room to get ready for George that night. I could smell the perfume coming from her window when I sat in the yard watching Mother hang the clothes up. I could hear Aunt Mae singing, too, but none of them were songs I knew. Except for one, and that was one

I'd heard coming from the barroom in town when Mother and I passed it once going shopping. I never knew how Aunt Mae learned it. When I asked her, she said her nurse had sung it to her when she was a little girl. But I knew that nurses never sang like that.

I didn't like George from the first time I saw him. His hair was long and gray, and it was always greasy. There were red marks all over his face, and it was a very lean one. He stood pretty straight for being about seventy. His eyes were shifty and never looked straight at you. In the first place, I was mad at him because he took almost all of Aunt Mae's time away from me. He never paid much attention to me, but I remember when one night I was sitting in the living room and he was waiting for Aunt Mae he said I looked like a very tender one, and he pinched me so hard on the arm that the spot was colored for a week. I was always too afraid of him to scream, but I screamed at him enough in my dreams when I would see him riding my train over me as I was tied to the track.

He carried on with Aunt Mae all through that summer and into part of the fall. Aunt Mae never spoke of marriage, so I didn't know why he was courting her, because all that normally leads to marriage somehow or other. I knew that Mother and Poppa weren't feeling so easy about it as they had been. At night when Aunt Mae and George were on the porch or out for a walk, I would sit with them in the kitchen and listen to them talk. Mother told Poppa that she didn't like George and that he was up to no good and things like that, and Poppa just told her that she was silly, but I could understand that he was wondering too.

One night Aunt Mae and George went for a walk in the

hills and didn't return until about six in the morning. I couldn't sleep that night, so I was sitting at my window, and I saw them come into the yard. They didn't talk to each other, and George left without even telling Aunt Mae good night, or maybe good morning. Mother and Poppa never found out. I was the only one who knew, but I didn't say anything. I saw Aunt Mae pass by my bedroom when she came upstairs, and there were leaves all tangled in the back of her hair. I thought maybe she fell down.

About a month after that, we never saw George anymore, and Mother told me he left town. I didn't think anything about it. As a matter of fact, I was happy, because now Aunt Mae and I could be together more. But it changed her. She never took me walking on the street anymore. She only played in the yard. She wouldn't even go around the block to the drugstore but sent me there to buy what she wanted. Poppa and Mother didn't invite friends over much anymore, or maybe they didn't want to come. I got used to staying right in the yard and began to work up quite an imagination with my cars. Now it was Aunt Mae who was the slow one. Sometimes she'd just stare up over the trees for a long while, and I'd have to nudge her and tell her it was her turn to move her truck. Then she'd smile and say, "Oh, I'm sorry, David," and begin pushing it along. But she either went the wrong way or did something wrong so that I ended up playing by myself while she just sat and stared at some nothing in the sky. One day she got a letter from George, but she just tore it up when she took it out of the mailbox and read the handwriting. I found out it was from him when I got older and could read and found it taped together in her dresser drawer. I never read what it said, because I had been taught not to do that kind of thing, but I was always curious about it. In eighth grade I found out what happened. George hadn't really left town but had been arrested by the sheriff on a morals charge because some girl's mother made some kind of complaint.

So here I am riding on this train. It's still dark out except for neon signs we pass sometimes. The last town went by too fast for me to see the name. The clicking on the rails is getting faster, and I can see the trees crossing the moon quick now. The years before I went to school passed by just about as quick as those trees are passing by the moon.

# Two

Then we moved. Something went wrong at the factory and Poppa lost his job, so we had to move to an old farmhouse-like house up on a hill right where the town ended.

It was a tan and brown place, but the paint was so faded you couldn't tell what color it was at first. There were so many rooms that we locked plenty of them up and never used them, and the whole place made me think of the hotel down in town, except it wasn't quite so large. The furniture in the other house came with the price of the rent, so we really didn't have any of our own worth mentioning, just things like the toilet seat Aunt Mae bought when she said the old one pinched.

About the saddest place was the living room, really the front room, with only an old couch Mother got from some friends and two old-fashioned chairs of Aunt Mae's. At first

we didn't have any curtains, but Aunt Mae had some beautiful old stage costumes that she tore up to use instead. I can't
say that they looked bad, though, even if they weren't wide
or long enough for the big windows. Every window in the
front room had a different curtain. The big one that looked
onto the porch had one made out of an evening dress with
big pink roses and lace. On one of the smaller windows Aunt
Mae put a curtain she made out of a shroud she wore in
some murder play, and on the other one she had a red satin
costume from a minstrel show. When the sun came through
all three windows, it made the room so red and bright that
Poppa said it reminded him of hell, and he would never sit
with us in there. I think this was because the curtains were
Aunt Mae's costumes, too, and he didn't want the sun to
shine on him through them.

Upstairs in the bedrooms we had some old beds someone
had left in the house, and they were so hard and smelled so
much that I never fell asleep till I had tossed around for
about an hour. Anybody who got close to them could tell
that they must have been used by little children ever since
they were built. Aunt Mae got sick from the smell of her
mattress the first night we slept there. She slept on the couch
that night and then threw all of her powder on her bed the
next day.

Inside the house there wasn't much more to see, but you
could see almost the whole country from the front porch.
You could see our town down at the bottom of the hills, and
over from the side of the porch you could see the county seat
pretty well on clear days, and you could tell where it was
anytime if you looked for the factory smokestack, because it
was painted orange. There was a big black mark on it that

was a big R when you got close to it. It stood for Renning, the people who owned the factory. I always remember the smokestack because Poppa would sit on the porch and look at it and say, "Those Rennings are the people that are keeping us poor. Damn those rich buggers. They're the ones keeping this whole valley poor, them and the damn politicians they get elected to run us." His work wasn't too steady now, and he sat on the porch most of the time and looked out over the county.

Our own yard was just cinders and a few weeds that grew around the steps and the porch. It was hard to play in the yard because there wasn't much to do, and if I fell down on the cinders they'd stick in my skin and have to be washed out with soap. I couldn't play back in the hills either, because they were full of snakes, so I got used to playing on the porch and in the house. The only time the cinders were fun was when it rained. Then you could pack them tight like cement and make dams, which was easy to do with all the water that came down from the hills when it rained.

Rain was something we were always afraid of at the hill house. After we moved there, we heard that the other people left years before because the house was too dangerous when it rained. Of course the roof gave trouble, not having been taken care of in so long, but the real trouble was with the foundations. The hills were nothing but clay, and when the rain came down them, the foundations would sink in the soft mud. That's why the cinders were in the yard, so that you could walk around there after a rain. If you went back into the hills after a rain, though, you had to wear boots.

When I first looked at the house, I could tell it was leaning and not straight, but it wasn't until after the first spring we were there and the first real rain came that we knew why. All night that night the house rumbled, and we thought it was just the thunder. In the morning the kitchen had dropped down on one side and there was wet clay under the stove. We had plenty of empty rooms downstairs, so we made another room the kitchen and left the old one just dropping there at the back of the house in a crazy way. When the hurricanes came in off the Atlantic that fall, we lost that old room and half of the front porch too.

I set up my train in one of the empty rooms upstairs, and I made all kinds of scenery for it to pass through. I made a tunnel and a hill out of some old boxes, and made a bridge with some of the trellis that was nailed to the front porch for climbing roses. Everyone could tell that climbing roses would never grow in that clay and cinders. It made Aunt Mae mad, though, because she liked the trellis and said that she could sit and imagine there were roses on it, even if there weren't.

My train was a beautiful thing, though. It ran all through the room. First it went under the tunnel, then over an old shoe box which I covered with crepe paper to make it look like a green hill, then it came down off the shoe box over the trellis bridge, which looked just like the steel bridge they had over the river at the county seat. From there it had a clear stretch over the floor in a circle and stopped back at the tunnel.

The same fall that we had the hurricane off the Atlantic was the fall I entered County Elementary. That was the name of the grade school down in town. It was far from our place. In the morning I had to go down the hill and across town to get to it, because it was at the foot of the range of hills opposite from ours. When it rained, I wore my boots to get off the hill. Then I had to carry them with me through town, and they were always wet and covered with clay, and they'd get me dirty and ruin my homework papers.

The school was a wooden building in the middle of a big yard that didn't have any grass on it. It had four rooms. I went into the first, second, and third room, but they had a fourth, fifth, and sixth room and also a seventh and eighth. I don't know what the last room was used for, but a big boy told me what happened there sometimes at night when he and his friends used it, and I didn't understand what he was talking about.

There were three teachers, two women and a man. The man had the seventh and eighth room. He was from out of state, but the two women were from town. One was our neighbor when we lived in town, and she didn't like Aunt Mae. I got her for my first teacher.

She recognized me right away and asked if the hussy was still living with us. I asked her what she meant, and she said that I should stop trying to pull her leg, that she knew my smart-aleck kind, that I was a perfect nephew for Aunt Mae, sly and tricky. When she said "sly and tricky," it sounded like the kind of words the preacher at church used, and I didn't like him. Her name was Mrs. Watkins. I knew her husband too, because he was a deacon at the church. I don't know what he did for a living, but his name was always in the paper trying to make the county dry, trying to keep the colored people from voting, trying to take *Gone with the Wind* out of the county library because so many people were reading it and he just knew it was "licentious." Someone wrote a letter to the paper asking if Mr. Watkins had ever read the book, and Mr. Watkins answered it saying that no, he would never lower himself to such a degree, that he "just knew" it was dirty because they were going to make a movie of it and therefore it had to be dirty, and that the man who had questioned his activities was an "agent of the devil." All this made the people of the county respect him, and a group met in front of the library in black masks and went in and took *Gone with the Wind* off the shelf and burned it on the sidewalk. The sheriff didn't want to do anything about it because he'd get into too much trouble with the people in town, and anyway, the election was next month.

Mrs. Watkins knew how the people felt about her husband after he did this to protect county morals, and whenever someone played around in the room, she'd say that she was going to talk to Mr. Watkins and see what he would do to punish such a person. This made all the playing in the room stop, because we were afraid Mr. Watkins would do to us what he did to the book. Anyway, at lunch one day the little boy who sat next to me told me that he was positive Mr. Watkins would burn anyone who was bad in his wife's room. After this really got around, Mrs. Watkins had the quietest room you've ever heard, and it was the wonder of the other two teachers, because when someone finished three years so quiet in Mrs. Watkins', he just naturally got a lot noisier in the next room.

Because she said I was a bad influence, Mrs. Watkins made me sit in the front row "right under her eye," as she said. This made me mad at Aunt Mae, but then I realized I was happy that she hadn't been friendly with Mrs. Watkins. I knew no one could be unless he was a deacon or a member of the Ladies' Aid, and Aunt Mae didn't like that kind either.

After a few days I began to notice that Mrs. Watkins was cross-eyed. That was something I had never noticed before, and when I told Aunt Mae, she laughed and laughed and said she hadn't noticed it either.

I memorized Mrs. Watkins' whole body the first week, along with a few pages out of the primer reader. Where I sat, my head came just a little above her knee, and I never felt a bonier knee in my life. I was just looking at her legs and wondering why she never shaved them the way Mother and Aunt Mae did when she hit me on the chin with her knee and told me to pay attention. My front tooth had been loose for a week, but I had been too afraid to let Mother or Poppa pull it out. When Mrs. Watkins' knee hit, I felt it pop loose and I let out a little "ouch," which I think pleased her. She didn't know she had done me a favor, and I never told her. I kept the tooth in my mouth until after class, then I spat it out and kept it, and I looked in the mirror at home and saw the new one coming through.

I wondered why a woman had such a straight body, because both Mother and Aunt Mae were round, and you could lay against them and be comfortable. Mrs. Watkins was straight all the way, with two big bones sticking out near her neck. You never knew where her waist was. Some days her dress would make it look like it was at her hips, but then it would be up across her chest or else near to where a waist should be. She must have had a big navel, because thin dresses sank way in near her stomach.

One day she was bending down over my desk to correct a paper, and I smelled her breath for the first time. I didn't know where I'd smelled that smell before, but I knew I had. I turned my head away and tried to cover my nose with my reader. That didn't do any good, though, and I could still smell it on the way home. It was a kind of odor you can't forget, the kind that reminds you of something or someone, like the smell of flowers always reminds me of funerals.

I don't know what I learned that year with Mrs. Watkins, but whatever it was there wasn't much of it, and I didn't like what there was. With three classes in the same room, she could only spend a little time with each one. I do know that I learned to read a little, because the next summer when I went to the movies with Aunt Mae I could read the name of the movie and people in it pretty well. I could add, too, and knew how to print. Poppa said that was all I had to know and I didn't have to go back the next fall. That was alright by me, but Mother wouldn't let me listen to him. Poppa was trying to grow some crops back in the hills above the house, and he needed someone to help him plow the clay, and Mother said that was why he didn't want me to go back to school.

When I heard that, I was glad to return in the fall, even if it was to Mrs. Watkins. Poppa couldn't grow anything in the hills, and Mother knew it. Anything was better than having him sit on the porch all the time the way he did. He was working part-time down in town at a gas station, but the hours were short, and when he came home he just sat there on the porch and looked onto the town and back into the hills. I thought he was crazy when he said he was going to start farming up in the hills. When the clay hardened after a rain, it was like cement, and anyone would know that no seeds would be able to come through. Aunt Mae had tried to start a garden behind the house, but when she didn't have time to water it, the mud got hard and began to crack just like it did all through the hills.

He spent all one week's salary, and it wasn't much, to buy some seeds and a little plow that a man could work by himself. He got a rake, too, and a shovel and a little hatchet to cut the small pines that grew all over. I was sitting in the front room doing my spelling for Mrs. Watkins the night he came home with all this. It was the regular pay night, and Mother had only some hush puppies and fried fish because it was near the end of the week and we didn't have any money in the house. I had twenty-three cents in my bank, but Mother wouldn't ever take that even though I had told her she could have it.

Aunt Mae was still upstairs, probably still sleeping from her afternoon nap. The sun was setting right behind the Renning smokestack, which looked like a black matchstick in front of an orange lightbulb. The sunset made the room look all orange, except for the bright light I was studying by. Outside I heard Poppa coming across the cinders in the front yard, making the heavy crunching sound that he always did, and there was a lighter crunch behind him. I saw him carrying some bags over his shoulder. Behind him was a colored boy with some big things wrapped in hardware paper. Poppa took these, and the boy went off across the cinders down to town.

"Mother." I put my pencil down on my copybook. "Poppa's here."

I heard the fish frying back in the kitchen as she opened the door into the front room.

"Good, David." She was wiping the greasy cornmeal on her apron. "He has his money with him."

She hurried to the door and met him as he was about to open the door.

"Oh, Frank, what's all that?" She looked at the bags over his shoulder and the big wrapped packages on the steps.

He walked past her and threw the bags on the floor near the kitchen door.

"Seeds, Sarah, seeds."

"Seeds? What are they for? Frank, are you really going through with that crazy plan to grow things on the hill? What did you buy them with?"

"With the money I got paid at the gas station. All of it." He turned away and started to go up the stairs, but Mother grabbed his arm, and a terrible scared look came into her eyes.

"All of it? All of the gas station money, Frank? No, no, you couldn't do that, not for seeds that are never going to grow. What are we going to eat this week? There's no more food in the house."

He went up two more steps, but Mother grabbed him again.

"Damn it, let me go. I can spend my money like I want. There's money to be made back in the hill, do you hear me, plenty money."

"But you can't use the money we live on to go after it, Frank. Take those seeds back to town tonight and get the money back." Mother was hanging on to the cuff of his shirt. She was frightened now to let go of him.

"Get off me. Damn it to hell, get off. You can always get food for this week. Go sell some of Mae's jewelry down at the barroom. There's some women upstairs there that like that kind of stuff. Let me go!"

"Frank, you fool, you stupid fool. You have a son to feed. I can take anything you say, go ahead and say it. Call Mae what you want to. I know what you think of her. I just need the money. We have to eat. We can't sit and starve and wait for a few seeds to work where even trees can hardly grow. There's still time to get down to town and get your, our, money back. Oh, Frank, please, please."

I saw Poppa's knee coming up, and I called out for Mother to get off the stairs. She was crying and didn't hear me, and Poppa's knee was already at her chin. She screamed and rolled backward down the stairs. I got to her just as she reached the floor. The blood was already flowing out the sides of her mouth.

When I looked up, Poppa was gone, and since he hadn't passed me, he must have gone upstairs. Aunt Mae was coming down the stairs to where Mother and I were. Her eyes were wide.

"David, what happened?" she called. She didn't come any lower, and I thought it must have been the blood on Mother's chin that frightened her. She was afraid of blood or anything like that.

"Aunt Mae, come down quick. Mother's hurt, and I don't know what to do." Mother was moaning and rolling her head from side to side. Aunt Mae was crying now. The noise must have got her up, because her hair was all loose and hanging in her face, and through her tears I could see her eyes all sleepy and surprised.

"You must call a doctor, David, that's all. I wouldn't know what to do for her." She began to cry harder, and it made me feel frightened.

"But you can just help me to move her, Aunt Mae, then I can call the doctor."

"Alright, David, I'll come down, but forget about the doctor. I don't think there's any money in the house to pay him with."

Aunt Mae came down the stairs shaky. Her face was white, and her hands couldn't keep a hold on the rail. She took Mother's feet, and I took the head, and we moved her to the old sofa in the front room. Mother moaned and kept rolling her head.

"Look in her mouth, Aunt Mae, that's where it's bleeding from." I was holding Aunt Mae by the arm because she was about to go back upstairs.

"No, David, no. I don't know what to do. I'm scared. She might be dying."

"Just look in her mouth, Aunt Mae. That's where the blood is coming from." I must have really looked anxious, or half mad, if someone can look that way at seven years old. Anyway, Aunt Mae stopped pulling away from me and said, "Alright."

She opened Mother's mouth and stuck her finger slowly in. At that moment Mother moaned again and closed her teeth. Aunt Mae screamed and pulled her finger out fast. When she had quieted down enough, she stuck it back in again and said, "I don't know, David, but all I can see and feel is that a tooth has been knocked out. Let's pray that it isn't anything more."

Later, when we had Mother upstairs, Aunt Mae got around to asking me what started all this. I began to tell her, but I remembered Poppa hadn't passed me on the stairs earlier. I jumped up and started going through all the upstairs rooms. Poppa was nowhere, so I went back to Mother's room and told Aunt Mae that Poppa was gone.

"When I heard all the crying and noise, I got out of bed

and was almost knocked down by your father running through my room. He went out the window onto the porch roof," Aunt Mae told me as she changed the ice pack on Mother's cheek to another place. Mother hadn't come around yet, but she was mumbling and her eyes were flittering.

Then I wondered what had happened to Poppa. I didn't want to see him again, but I was curious to know where he had gone. I went downstairs and onto the porch. All his things that he bought were gone. The moon was shining so white on the cinders in the yard that they were shining like diamonds. It was a still night in the valley, and the pines on the hill were swaying just ever so slightly. Down in town people's lights were going off in their windows, leaving only a few neon lights on Main Street still burning. I could see the big neon Bible all lighted up on the preacher's church. Maybe it's lighted up tonight, too, with its yellow pages and red letters and big blue cross in the center. Maybe they light it up even if the preacher isn't there.

I could see the old section where we used to live, even the exact house. There was somebody new living in it now. I thought about how lucky they were to have a nice house in town without cinders in their yard and four feet of clay under that. Mrs. Watkins lived next door. All the lights were out there. She always told us how early she went to bed. She never had any fighting in her house. She got a nice check from the state for teaching school, too, so she never had to fight with her husband over that.

I leaned back against the porch post and looked at the sky. All the stars were there. It was such a clear night that you could even see some that you only saw about once or twice a year. My legs were beginning to get cold from the air that was setting in, and I wished I was old enough to wear long pants. I felt little and small from the cold and the stars, and I was frightened about what was going to happen to us with Poppa gone. My nose began to hurt in the tip. All of a sudden the stars got all blurry as the tears filled up my eyes, and then I began to shake hard from the shoulders, and I put my head on my knees and cried and cried.

The last neon sign on Main Street was just going out when I got up to go into the house. My eyes felt funny because my lashes were stuck together and the lids were sore. I didn't lock the front door. Nobody in the valley ever locked their door at night or any other time. The seeds were gone from where Poppa had put them near the kitchen door, so he must have come to get them when Aunt Mae and I were upstairs taking care of Mother. I wondered if Poppa had gone forever. I wondered where he was now. Back in the hills, or maybe down in town somewhere.

All of a sudden I realized I was hungry. In the kitchen the hush puppies that Mother had made were on the table in a bowl. I sat down and ate some and drank a little water. The fish were in the pan where Mother turned off the fire when Poppa came in, but they were cold and greasy and didn't look very good. Over my head the one bulb that hung from the electric cord was pretty greasy too, and it made long shadows after everything and made my hands look white and dead. I sat with my head in my hands and ran my eyes over the design in the oilcloth on the table again and again. I watched the blue checks turn into the red and then into the black and back into the red again. I looked up at the light-bulb and saw blue and black and red checks before my eyes.

In my stomach the hush puppies were heavy. I wished I hadn't eaten anything.

Upstairs Aunt Mae was covering Mother as I came into the room.

"She'll be alright, David," Aunt Mae said when she saw me in the doorway. I looked at Mother, and she seemed to be sleeping.

"What about Poppa, Aunt Mae?" I was leaning on the door.

"Don't worry about him. There's nowhere else for him to go. We'll have to take him back when he shows up, though I can't say how I want to."

It surprised me to hear Aunt Mae talk like that. I'd never heard her talk sensible that way before. I always thought she was afraid of Poppa, and here she was deciding what to do about him. I felt proud of her. She made me lose some of the frightened feeling I had. Behind her the moonlight was shining into the room so that it made her look all silvery around the edges. Her hair was down on her shoulders, and the light made every separate hair shine like a spider's web in the sun.

Aunt Mae looked big and strong. Just standing there, she looked like a big statue to me, a silver one, like the one in the park in town. She was the only one in the house that could help me, the only strong person older than I was. I ran to her all of a sudden and stuck my head in her stomach and held my arms tight around her back. She felt soft and warm and like something I could hold on to that would take care of me. I felt her hand on my head, petting me softly. I squeezed her tighter until my head went in her stomach so much that it hurt her.

"David"—she ran her hand down my back—"Are you afraid? Everything will be alright. When I was on the stage, I was hurt worse than you are now. I was never really very good, David, as an entertainer. I always knew that, but I loved the stage, and I loved to have the spotlights blinding me and the noise of a band under me. David, when you're on a stage and you're singing and you can feel the beat of the band shaking the boards on the stage, you feel like you're drunk. Yes, you do, baby. The stage was like liquor to me, like beer or whiskey. It hurt me at times, just like liquor hurts a drunk man, but it hurt me in my heart, that's what made it different. I was lucky whenever I got a job in some little dance hall in Mobile or Biloxi or Baton Rouge. What did I get paid? Just enough to live in a cheap hotel and buy a new costume now and then.

"There were times, David, when I didn't know where my next meal was coming from. Then I went into the dime store in whatever town I was and got a job. The last few years they wouldn't even give me a job there because they want young girls, and I had to work as a cleanup woman in the hotel I was staying in to get enough money to leave town. Then I'd do the same thing in the next town usually.

"I never sang good, honey, but when I was younger at least I was better-looking. Sometimes I could get a job just because I looked good in my clothes. The men liked me then. They came just to see me, and I went out a lot. They made promises, and I believed the first few, but after I saw how I was fooled, I was hurt, hurt so that I thought my heart would break. Then I couldn't hope to be honest to any man by letting him marry me, because you see, he'd be getting a used-up piece of goods, so to speak. After that there was nothing but my career, and that was slowing down. I couldn't take any more after those last ten years. No one would give me a job, not even some of those men who had made promises to me. The ones I had given so much to wouldn't answer the phone when I called. They had all married other girls and had grandchildren. Those were the times when I sat in my hotel rooms and cried on the smelly pillows. All the other women my age could look out their kitchen window and see the wash drying on the line, but all I could see out my hotel window was a dirty alley full of old papers and lushes' broken wine bottles and garbage cans and cats and dirt. Was I hurt then, David? I wanted to commit suicide with the old rusty razor blades in those cheap bathrooms. But I wouldn't let those other people make me kill myself.

"The last job I had before I came to live with you all was in a real dump in New Orleans. I don't know why the man hired me, because he was a real tough dago with an eye on the cash register. He had about five girls he got from the bayous around town who did strips. They took their clothes off while three or four hopheads played some music. He got a lot of seamen from the boats in town for customers. They sat right under the stage and grabbed at the girls' ankles while they danced, or moved around, anyway, because they were just Cajun girls who came to the city on a promise and fell for it the way I did once.

"It was my second night there, and I didn't feel like going on because the musicians were so full of dope they played my music all wrong the night before. I had to keep the job, though, because I owed on my room and I needed some cash. When I went out, the lights were on me and the music was beating, and I felt better. The sailors were noisy that night like always, but there was one big one sitting near the door who began to laugh and call at me when I started singing. I was just going into the second chorus when I hear the dago shout from behind the bar, 'Watch out, Mae!' Before I knew what he was yelling about, I felt something hit me hard on the head. It turned out that sailor threw a beer bottle at me, a big, thick brown thing. Those Cajun girls were so good to me, honey. They paid for the doctor who brought me to and fixed my head, and they paid the hotel and got me a train ticket when I said I wanted to come here.

"I was hurt that all those years ended that way. I wanted to be happy with you all here, but I've made the people in the town hate me, and I didn't want for that to happen. I've always dressed bright, and maybe I went on the stage to show off, but no one ever paid any attention to me in the cities. Here I've been just a sore thumb, David, you know that. I know what they think of me here, and I didn't want them to.

"I never told anyone these things, David, not even your mother. Maybe it was good to save them for now when I could show you how small your hurt is next to all the ones I have."

I looked up into Aunt Mae's face. I couldn't make out the expression on it in the shadows, but the moonlight shining on her cheeks showed how wet they were. I felt a warm drop fall on my forehead, and it tickled as it ran down my face, but I didn't move to wipe it off.

"Come on, David, you can sleep with me tonight. I feel lonely."

We went to Aunt Mae's room, and she helped me take off

my clothes. I waited by her window while she put on her nightgown which she always wore. I felt her come up beside me.

"David, do you pray every night before you go to sleep?"

I told Aunt Mae that I did sometimes, and I wondered why she wanted to ask me a question like that. I didn't think she ever thought about praying.

"Come kneel with me by the window, David, and we'll pray that your mother feels well tomorrow and that nothing happens to your Poppa tonight and that you and I . . . that you and I won't be hurt too bad tomorrow or ever again."

That seemed like a beautiful prayer, so I looked out the window and began, and my eye fell on the neon Bible below and I couldn't go on. Then I saw the stars in the heaven shining like the beautiful prayer, and I began again, and the prayer came out without even thinking, and I offered it up to the stars and the night sky.

# Three

The next morning Aunt Mae got me up and dressed me for school. Mother was alright, but she was still sleeping, so Aunt Mae said she'd make me some breakfast. I never saw Aunt Mae do anything in the kitchen, and I wondered what she was going to fix. While I was washing my face, I heard her getting ready downstairs, slamming the icebox and walking back and forth in the kitchen.

When I came down, the food was on the table. She had a pile of biscuits in a bowl, so I took one and began to butter it. The bottom was all burnt, and the inside was still wet dough. I was hungry, though, because all I had the night before was the water and hush puppies. She brought a pan to the table with some brown fried eggs floating around in about two inches of fat. There was such a proud look on her face that I said, "Oh, Aunt Mae, those look good," when I saw them.

That made her happy, and we sat and ate the eggs and biscuits like they were real fine.

I got my books and the lunch Aunt Mae made for me and left for school. There were a lot of things on my mind. Where was Poppa? I thought he'd be back at the house in the morning, but I hadn't said anything to Aunt Mae, and she didn't talk to me about it. Then I remembered that I didn't do the work in my copybook for Mrs. Watkins. I couldn't get in any more trouble with her, so I put my books and lunch down by the side of the path and got my pencil out and sat down. I could feel the seat of my pants getting wet from the dew on the grass, and I thought how funny that was going to look. With the copybook slipping off my knee every time I went to write a letter, the page began to look bad. My A's looked like D's, and sometimes my commas slid all the way down to the next line. I finally finished it and got up and pulled the little wet blades of grass off my pants.

I still had to get off the hill and cross town to get to school. The sun was up pretty well now. That meant that there wasn't too much time. Something felt heavy in my stomach, and I was sure it was those eggs and biscuits of Aunt Mae's. With the taste of the eggs still in my throat, I began to belch, and belch hard. Belching always made my throat feel hot, so I started to breathe the cool hill air through my mouth. It made me feel a little better, but the burning was still way down, in my chest, and it stayed there.

I got off the hill onto a street and decided to take the shortest way I could. It was the street right behind Main where they had all the little restaurants and mechanics' shops. Usually I went another way, through the pretty houses, because I liked it better.

Here they had old boxes in the gutter and old hubcaps and big garbage cans covered with flies that had such a strong smell I had to hold my nose when I passed. It was dark in the mechanics' places, with old cars on wooden blocks or bodies without wheels hanging from chains. The mechanics sat around in the doorways waiting for some business, and every word they spoke had "Christ" in it or "damn" or something like that. I wondered why Poppa had never been a mechanic, and thought that maybe he had been at one time, or maybe his father, because he never told me anything about his family, my grandpeople.

The mechanics' places were mostly tin garages with old oilcans out in front and in the alleys. When it rained there, the water in the gutters was never clear but had purple and green colors on it that made any kind of design you wanted when you moved the water with your finger. I don't think the mechanics ever shaved, and I wondered how they got all the grease off their skin when they went home at night.

There was one of those little restaurants between almost every mechanic's shop. They were named the DeLux Kitchen or Joe's or Kwik-Meal or Mother Eva's or other names like that. In front of every one there was a blackboard with the food they were having for the day, and it was always something like beans with rice or pork chops with beans or beans and chicken. I never knew how they could sell food so cheap, because there wasn't any meal that cost more than fifty cents. It must have been that they didn't have to pay much for the buildings they used.

The barroom was on this street too. All along the front they had fake marble with neon lettering around the door and windows. I never saw what it looked like on the inside because it was always closed when I passed in the morning. I don't suppose anyone was meant to look above the first floor. The marble and neon stopped there, and the rest up to the roof was old weatherboards, brown and gray. There were three windows up there, big long ones that led onto a wooden balcony like all the old buildings in town had on the second floor. In the morning they were usually closed, but sometimes they were open and things were drying out on the balcony. They must have been women's underwear, but not like any I'd seen at home. They were made out of black lace with little shiny red rosebuds sewed on them in different places. Sometimes there were sheets hanging out too, or pillowcases or black net stockings like no one in town wore. When I got to Mr. Farney's room in school, I found out who lived there.

There were plenty empty lots along the street too, just like all over town. The only thing different was that they weren't kept clean like the others. They had big weeds in them, and sunflowers and wild violets. The mechanics threw their old oilcans and car parts in them when there wasn't enough room left in the alleys or the gutter. Next to the barroom they had one full of old rotting chairs and beer cases where about ten mangy cats lived. Of course the cats were all over here, in the empty lots and everywhere. They hung around the back doors of the diners for food, and you could always see them climbing in and out of the garbage cans with their ribs showing through their fur. I often thought of what a hard life these cats had and how if people only took care of them what nice pets they could be. They were always having kittens, but I knew what Poppa would do if I brought one home. Once I saw him throw a brick at a cat that was in our yard, a little one that I was trying to give some old meat to.

When I got to the end of this street, I just had to turn left to get to the school. The boys and girls were beginning to go in when I was about a block away, so I ran to be sure I wouldn't be late. My face was all red, and I was out of breath by the time I got to Mrs. Watkins'. I was the last one to take my seat, which was in the front row "right under her eye." She got down off her platform and came over to where I sat. I didn't look up at her, but my eye followed the pattern on her dress, a bouquet of faded flowers.

"Well, class, we have someone who just got here on time today."

I thought I could make out one of the flowers to be a daisy.

"He's one of the poor folks that lives up in the hills and don't have the money to buy an alarm clock."

Some of her pets in the class giggled—the preacher's daughter by his first wife, her niece, the boy who stayed after school to beat out the erasers. Now I saw that the flower wasn't a daisy but really a white rose. She hit me with her knee.

"Get up."

I stood up, and then everyone began to giggle, and I saw a terrible look come over Mrs. Watkins' face.

"What's everybody laughing at?"

She was mad at the whole class now, not only me, and then I remembered the seat of my pants and how it must have looked. Everyone stopped giggling and talking except her pets, who hadn't started in the first place. The boy who cleaned the erasers raised his hand. Mrs. Watkins nodded at him.

"Look at the back of him." He pointed at the wet of my pants.

I almost tried to pull my buttocks in when I heard him say

that, but Mrs. Watkins had already spun me around. She looked happy to me.

"What's the matter? Try to sleep in your clothes?"

Everybody screamed at this, even her pets, or maybe I should say, especially her pets. My throat was burning again, and all of a sudden I belched the loudest I'd ever heard anyone do it. Mrs. Watkins slapped me so hard I felt my head roll back on my shoulders. The ring she had from the auxiliary of the preacher's church made a small cut on my cheek. She was holding on to me by the arm.

"I've never had a pupil like you, son. You know, the state doesn't have to accept everyone into their schools. Did you know that? Well, you might find out about it soon enough. Come with me."

She grabbed my books and my lunch and took me with her to the empty room. I was frightened the way she looked at me. There were two or three old chairs in the room and an old desk. When she had closed the door, she pushed me into one of the chairs.

"I'm going to report you to the state authorities, do you hear that? They'll get you, son, they'll get you. I hope the Lord will be merciful with you for your behavior to those trying to instruct you in His path. You and your family are fallen-away Christians. You are not on the church rolls anymore. I see that. I see all those things. You may remain in this room to meditate on your failings, and you will not leave until I come for you."

She closed the door and left. I knew we didn't go to the preacher's anymore because we didn't have any money to pay the church pledge. I wondered what she was going to do with me about the state authorities. Would I be put out of school because of Aunt Mae's eggs? I tried to be mad at Aunt Mae, but I couldn't. I just hoped that when I was put out of school they never told Aunt Mae why. She was probably belching at home right now, and she'd know.

I was wondering how long Mrs. Watkins was going to leave me in the room, too. The pants were beginning to dry, but the wet had soaked through and it was uncomfortable. I wanted to be outside in the sun where they could dry quicker through to my skin. There were two windows in the room, but one had no glass in it. A little air came through that one, so I tried to open the other, but it wouldn't move.

After a while I got used to the smell in the room, but at first I didn't know what to make of it. I looked all around and saw some old wine bottles in one corner, and I picked one up and smelled its sweet strong odor. But that wasn't the only thing making the whole room smell the way it did. I can't say what it smelled like. There was a little of the old wine smell, but there were other ones too. It smelled musty and dirty, and yet that cheap kind of perfume Aunt Mae used was there, and the smell of a cigarette and a leather jacket. Something was grating under my foot, and when I lifted it, the thing was a bobby pin. I knew none of the girls in school used bobby pins except some of the big ones in Mr. Farney's room.

Through the door I could hear Mrs. Watkins down the hall in class, and I heard Mr. Farney's funny high voice too. Miss Moore's classes were out on a field trip into the hills to get some clay for modeling. There was a lock on the door, so I locked it and took my clothes off and hung my pants on one of the chairs to dry. It felt good to be naked, but I knew that no one better find me like that.

The sun was really up and coming in bright and strong through the open window. I had never stood naked in the sunlight, so I went to the window and let the yellow light fall on me. My body looked pale white except for my arms and face, and the breeze blew cool all around me.

I stood there for a long time looking out at the trees up on the hill and the blue sky with only a few clouds above the tallest pines. They moved slowly along, and I watched one all the way till it went behind the hill. I made one out to look like Aunt Mae's face, then it turned into a witch and then into what looked like an old man with a beard before it passed away.

Suddenly I felt someone's eyes on me, and there was a woman on the sidewalk with a bag of groceries staring at me. I jumped away from the window to get my clothes. They were dry, so I put them on. When I went back to the window she was gone, and I looked down the block and couldn't see her. I wondered where she went and if she saw me well. No one ever saw me naked but Aunt Mae and Mother and Poppa. Maybe the doctor when I was born, and the nurses, and once when I went to the doctor to have him look at me. I don't know why, but it makes you feel funny to have someone see you naked, it makes you feel nasty, though it shouldn't.

Out in the yard I heard everyone coming out from their classes. I looked at the sun, and it was straight overhead, so it was lunchtime. I got out Aunt Mae's lunch from under my books. She had it wrapped in a piece of newspaper with a rubber band around it. There were a few of the old hush puppies Mother made the night before and a sandwich with a little piece of ham on it. She didn't put any butter on the sandwich, but there was a flower packed in the lunch from the little garden Aunt Mae had tried to grow. I knew it was the only flower that had come out from the little plants she had. It was only a few blue petals, and I don't know what kind it was because I'd never seen such a weak-looking flower before. I took it back to her when I went home. She was so glad to have it back and so proud of it that I thought how nice it was of her to put it in my lunch when she thought it was so valuable.

Mrs. Watkins came out into the yard with our class and sat on a bench near the flagpole. I sat at the window and ate my sandwich, but she never looked over at where I was. I wondered if she called the state yet about me. If she would have just looked at me I could tell what she was thinking, but she never did, she just sat there and talked to Mr. Farney, although I knew she didn't like him. Mr. Farney was surprised to have Mrs. Watkins talking to him, and he showed it on his face. She always talked to people about him. It helped to have Mrs. Watkins like you in town. Mr. Farney knew this, and he was agreeing with everything she said, at least that's the way it looked from where I sat. He looked so uneasy I felt sorry for him.

I finished my sandwich and hoped I was outside and not in trouble. I picked up Aunt Mae's flower, and it smelled nice but faint. It seemed like such a wrong flower to be hers. Aunt Mae was more like a big bright sweet-smelling flower to me. A red one, maybe, that had a strong smell like honeysuckle, but not quite so innocent.

After a while someone rang the bell, and everyone went inside again. I heard them moving along the halls outside the door in the sort of steady file of thump-thump that the classes always made. When it all got quiet, the teachers' voices began again, Mrs. Watkins' through the nose, Miss Moore's, whose class had returned, sort of sweet, and Mr. Farney's high and trailing. The sun was getting lower. I wondered if the people from the state were coming. They probably were at the capital, and it would naturally take a while to get to town.

It seemed like a day later when I heard school letting out. When the boy who cleaned Mrs. Watkins' erasers finally left, I heard her coming down the hall. I wondered if she had the state people with her, but there was only one set of footsteps. She walked so slow toward the room that I prayed she'd hurry up and get it over with. All of a sudden she was rattling the doorknob, and then I remembered I forgot to take the lock off.

"Unlock this door."

I jumped up and ran and pulled at the lock, but she was leaning against the door, and I couldn't move it.

"I'll give you one second to get this lock off. One second!"

I was so scared I couldn't speak to tell her to stop pushing on the door.

"You don't think I can knock this door down to get in, do you, you little devil? Well, I hear you in there fooling with the door. I'll come in there and get you if it's the last thing I do today!"

She must have moved back from the door to throw herself against it, because the lock slipped and I pulled the door open. Mrs. Watkins came flying into the room. She must have expected to fall against the closed door, and she came in so fast with such a strange look on her face and her arms folded. She couldn't protect herself with her arms and fell over a chair onto the floor.

Before I could run away, she was up and had me by the collar. My heart was in my throat when I saw the horrible look on her face. Her cheek was red where she fell on it, and I could just see her little slit eyes full of tears through all the hair over her face. For a minute she just held me and breathed hot over me in quick, heavy breaths.

I could see the pain in her eyes. At least, that's all I could make her expression out to be. When she opened her lips they were still half closed and almost stuck to each other they were so dry. At first she had been pulling at my collar, but now she was leaning on my shoulders with all her weight. Her big bony body was almost bent in half.

"Get the doctor, go get him right away. Damn you, hurry!"

I ran out of the room and heard Mrs. Watkins fall on the floor moaning. Never before in my life did I run as fast. The doctor was over on Main Street three blocks away. I ran through people's backyards and got caught in clotheslines and frightened little children who were playing in the mud.

When I told the doctor, he kited over to the school. I was hot and tired and walked back slowly. Some kids in the neighborhood saw the doctor running over to the school and followed him. When I got back there, they had almost more people around than in the whole town. The ones in my class were laughing and making jokes about Mrs. Watkins, but I didn't feel like making jokes. I felt sick. Some asked me if I had done it, and I just didn't say anything.

When I got to the empty room, they were just putting Mrs. Watkins on a stretcher. She moaned all the while and really screamed when they gave the final lift. I stood there and looked at her and felt sorry to see anyone who was so powerful suddenly be so weak and afraid. She saw me and motioned for me to come near the stretcher. When I got near, I saw the scared look in her face wasn't all from pain. She grabbed ahold of my head and whispered in my ear.

"Don't ever dare to tell anyone a word about this. You can get into plenty trouble if you do. Understand?" Her finger- nails were digging into the flesh at the back of my neck. Her breath was hot and had the same bad smell. "Never a word to anyone."

I nodded, half out of relief, and wondered why Mrs. Watkins had told me to be quiet. I thought I'd have to beg her to have mercy on me. I was a lot older when I learned what the State Board of Education would have done to her if I ever opened my mouth. When I think of how grateful I was then, it makes me laugh.

After they took Mrs. Watkins out, I got my copybook and Aunt Mae's flower and left. A few people were still hanging around the school talking about the accident, which was now made out to be that Mrs. Watkins just tripped over a chair. The town people would have believed anything Mrs. Wat- kins said—that is, almost everyone except the newspaper editor, who was a pretty smart man from some college up east. When he wrote about the accident in a sort of sus- picious way, there was talk that Mr. Watkins was going to get up a petition against him. It never came around, though, because I guess Mr. Watkins realized the newspaper was the only way he could put himself before the town people.

Some old ladies stopped me and told me what a fine lad I was to run for the doctor and show such concern for Mrs. Watkins' welfare. The news about me was all over town by the time I got to Main Street. People who recognized me stopped and patted me on the head and kept me so long that it was dark by the time I got to the foot of the hill.

Then I remembered about Poppa and got to thinking about him and if he came home. The early stars were out. The moon was near the top of the hill as I looked up, and it was full and bright. It made the path and the leaves look silver, something like the early snow. Some night birds were already singing way up in the pines. One went *che-woot, che-woot, che-woot* in a long-drawn-out way that sounded like a dying person. I could hear that song ring out all over the hills as the other birds picked it up. Two or three flew across the moon going to meet some others in the tall pines on the north side of the valley. I wished I could fly and follow those birds and be two hundred feet above the hills and see into the next valley where I'd never been. Then I'd look back on the town from on top of the Renning smokestack. I'd look over the new town, too, and see all the new buildings I'd never seen and the streets I'd never walked on.

Nighttime was the time for all the little animals that lived in the hills to come out. They ran across the path every now and then, and sometimes I'd almost trip over one of them. It was strange that they were so scared of people when their real enemies were others of their own kind. I wasn't mad at them, because I knew what it was like to be scared to your bones by someone, only I felt a little sorry for them because I didn't have to worry about my enemy anymore.

When I got to the house it was all lighted up and Aunt Mae was sitting on the porch. I kissed her and gave her the flower, and she looked at it like it was her baby. The first thing I asked her was if Poppa was home.

She looked up from the flower and said, "Yes, he came home. He's still out in the dark behind the house trying to plow the land. Mother's got some food in the kitchen."

Aunt Mae followed me into the house and asked why I was so late. I didn't tell her the truth, but I told her that I got the doctor for Mrs. Watkins when she tripped over a chair and how people stopped to congratulate me. Aunt Mae beamed all over and said she was proud of me, even though Mrs. Watkins had hurt her many times.

Mother looked a little weak, but she was glad to see me. I didn't think there would be anything in the house to eat after what I heard her say to Poppa. She said he sold some of his seeds and the rake, and that bought a little food. She was silent after a while. When Aunt Mae told her about me at school, she said, "That's nice," and got quiet again.

All the time I ate she just stared at the wall and ran her finger along the oilcloth. Aunt Mae seemed to understand that she didn't want to speak, so I didn't say anything either. It was one of the quietest meals I ever ate, but it didn't make me sad. I was thinking that Mrs. Watkins had told me about the state authorities just to scare me and was planning to come into the empty room to really take care of me herself. I wondered what she would have done to me if she didn't hurt herself. I wondered what she was doing right then in the hospital. Well, anyway, I wasn't going to visit her to find out.

After a while I heard Poppa coming up the back steps. As soon as she heard him, Mother jumped up from the table and went upstairs. Just as he opened the back door, I heard one close above me. Poppa went over to the sink and washed his hands, and soon there was clay all over the faucet and thick tan water flowing into the drain. He wiped his hands on a dishcloth and went over to the stove. While he was looking in the pots I looked at Aunt Mae, and she was staring into the cup in front of her without any kind of look on her face. He filled up a plate and came and sat down at the table. He looked at me and said hello, and I nodded at him and tried to talk, but when I opened my mouth nothing came out of my throat. I felt embarrassed and wished I was upstairs with my train or out on the front porch or anywhere but where I was.

Aunt Mae must have seen the look on my face, because she said, "Let's go out front," and we left the kitchen. I sat on the steps, and Aunt Mae sat in a chair on the porch, the one she was sitting in when I came home. Mrs. Watkins' home was dark down in town. There were no lights on, so Mr. Watkins must have been with her. I wondered if the state paid teachers when they were sick. Besides Mrs. Watkins not working, I thought of the hospital bills she was going to have to pay. I thought of how worried Mr. Watkins would be with his wife out of school. I wondered if he'd get a job somewhere in town.

Tonight wasn't like the night before when it had been so still in the valley. A breeze was starting that soon turned into a wind. It was nice to sit on the steps and watch the pines on the far hills swaying against the sky. I looked around at Aunt Mae. Her yellow hair was flying all over her eyes, but she didn't move to straighten it. Her eyes were on the town, I don't know exactly what part. They were just staring down on the town.

It got dark on the porch after the clouds began to cover the moon. Pretty soon there was just a white glow in the sky covered by gray smoke. You could see the shadows of the clouds on the hills moving fast across the valley. Soon the whole sky was full of gray smoke from the south, and it looked like the valley had a gray lid on it. A rumbling began at the far hill and spread across the sky until it shook the house. The sky lit up off and on like one of the signs on Main Street, except without color, just a silver glow. The kind of cool breeze that always comes before a rain started up, and soon I could hear the first big drops on the porch roof and feel them hitting my knees. They hit the clay with a steady thump and made the cinders shine.

Aunt Mae and I got up and went inside. I went up to my room and sat on my bed and looked out at the pines swaying in the rain and thought how a day that started out so bad ended up so well.

# Four

The war had been on for quite a while now when Poppa got his notice from the draft. He didn't have to go, but he more or less enlisted. Mother and I and Aunt Mae went down to the train to see him off, and when he left he kissed Mother and he cried, and I'd never seen a man cry before. The train pulled away, and we stood there and watched it go, and Mother kept looking long after it passed around the hill.

Most of the young men in town went away too. Some of them returned when the war was over, and some didn't. Down on the street behind Main Street most of the mechanics' shops were empty. A lot of drugstores and groceries were boarded up, with "Closed for the Duration" written on the windows. We put up a service flag on the front door just like almost everyone did. You could see them on any street, even the one north of town where all the rich people lived, but not too many there.

The town got to be a real quiet place. Then they built a war plant down by the river, not a big one, just a little propeller factory. A lot of the women in town got jobs there because the men were mostly gone. Aunt Mae was one of them, and she was made supervisor of a section. Every morning when I went down to school she walked into town with me, wearing slacks and a bandanna and carrying a metal lunch box. She was about the oldest woman working in the plant, but she had a better job than a lot of ones who were younger.

Mother stayed at home and took care of the little acre of things Poppa planted up in the hills. She said he mentioned it in every letter, for her to take care of it and write him about it. He had two rows of cabbage no bigger than baseballs, and the rest of the things I could never make out because they rotted underground when Mother forgot to dig them up.

By now I was out of fourth grade and had been in Miss Moore's class for almost a year and a half. Mrs. Watkins was back teaching first to third after she was out for six months. We passed each other in the hall every day, but we always looked in a different direction. I could tell when she was coming by the funny way her steps sounded from her limp. When she first returned, one of her legs was in a cast for a month. That was the one that looked so stiff and that she stepped on so lightly.

Miss Moore was a nice lady that you can't describe too well. There was nothing different about her from anyone else. We got along, though, and my grades were better than they ever were for Mrs. Watkins.

With nothing much for anyone to do with their fathers and husbands and boyfriends gone, the movies were where everyone went. Even on Sunday nights it was crowded, and that was when the preacher had his evening meeting. Mr. Watkins tried to get the moviehouse closed on Sundays at six, but the sheriff's brother owned it, and something happened to his petition. They had a lot of Technicolor movies playing that Mother and I and Aunt Mae liked. In town we got the movies about a month after they played in the capital, and the bill was changed three times a week. We saw a lot of black-and-white movies too, but Bette Davis seemed to be in every one of them. Mother and Aunt Mae liked her, and I heard them crying next to me when she played a twin who was drowning while the other twin pulled a ring from her finger so she could pretend she was the one who really drowned and marry the drowned one's boyfriend. They had Rita Hayworth too, but she was always in Technicolor, and her hair was the reddest I ever saw. We saw Betty Grable in this movie about Coney Island. It looked like a wonderful place, and Aunt Mae told me she had been there and that it was down on the Gulf.

After a while signs began to show up all over town about a revival that was coming. It wasn't sponsored by the preacher like he usually did, because he was mad about the attendance at his church. This seemed like a mistake to me, because the people in the town liked revivals and never missed one. They came from out of the hills too, and from the county seat, when the preacher had some evangelist every year.

Across Main Street they had a rope hung from a building on one side to a building on the other. From the rope hung a long canvas poster that read:

SALVATION! SALVATION!

Come hear a stirring message each and every
night.

BOBBIE LEE TAYLOR

of Memphis, Tennessee

TWO WEEKS!          TWO WEEKS!

2000 seat tent          Empty lot foot Main Street

STARTING MARCH 23 7:30 P.M.

The stores had signs in their windows too, so it was hard
not to know anything about it if you knew how to read. The
preacher was mad, and the town knew it. He didn't notice
the sign hanging over Main Street. He never looked at the
window displays where they had a sign. In the paper a few
days later there was a notice that starting March 23 and
continuing for two weeks the preacher was holding Bible
conferences at the church every night at seven-thirty and all
were invited to attend.

I knew no one in the valley was going to go to one of the
preacher's Bible conferences when they could go and hear
good music and have a better time at a revival. March 23 was
about two weeks off, and every day the preacher ran his ad
saying that he was going to have Bible experts from all over
talk on the Bible and explain the full meaning of the Scrip-
tures. And every day more big posters showed up all over
town telling about Bobbie Lee Taylor's great revival.

One day some colored men turned up in the empty lot at
the foot of Main and began clearing the stumps. It was right
next to the schoolhouse, so Miss Moore, who always liked to
take field trips, let us go outside to see what she called the

stumps' "root formation." We were watching the colored men for about an hour when the preacher came by and told them to get off the public lands or he'd get the sheriff after them. They got scared and dropped their tools and went off. The preacher looked at our class sitting under the trees for a minute and went off too.

The next day the colored men showed up again, but this time there was a white man with them. The preacher didn't show up, so by the time school was out all the stumps were out and the lot, which was more like a big field, was all cleared and level. Big trucks began to come the days after, all with "Bobbie Lee Taylor, Boy Who Has Seen the Light, Wonder Evangelist!" written on them in yellow letters with a black shadow on one side. The colored men brought poles and big sheets of canvas out of the trucks and began to set up the tent. It went up pretty high and covered almost the whole field when they were finished. The ropes they had tied to pegs in the ground came all the way into the schoolyard it was so big. When it was up a smaller truck came with sawdust to throw on the ground on the inside.

They left it like that for about a week before the chairs came, and every day at lunchtime and when school was out, the boys went into the tent and had fights throwing the sawdust at each other. Some girls came in too, but they were the big ones in Mr. Farney's room who liked to have the big boys throw them down in the sawdust, though they pretended it made them mad.

When school was out I'd go home with the sawdust sticking in my collar and itching me down my back where I couldn't get at it. You could see everyone coming out of the tent—a few at a time, because most didn't like to leave—

with sawdust in their hair and trying to reach down their backs to scratch. The big girls came out brushing it out of their long hair with their fingers and smoothing the wrinkles out of their skirts. All the way home they got pushed by the big boys, usually one girl between two boys. They would scream and laugh and try to run away, but not too hard.

The twenty-third was almost here. A truck came to the tent with the chairs, the wooden folding kind, and they made so much noise putting them up that Miss Moore couldn't teach the class. From the window we watched them take the chairs off the truck thin as a plank, then flip them open into full chairs.

Bobbie Lee Taylor came in on the twenty-second and talked over the radio and got his picture in the paper. I couldn't see what he looked like from the picture in the paper, because you couldn't make anyone out from those pictures unless it was President Roosevelt or someone else you knew well. They were so dark a person's eyes were big black spots and his hair looked like it met his eyebrows. Everyone looked the same except Roosevelt because his head was wide and Hitler because his hair hung down so you couldn't miss him.

The day of the revival almost everybody left school right after it let out. They were all going and had to get home to get ready. Mother and Aunt Mae hadn't talked about it, so I didn't think we were going. All the way home down Main Street the shops were closing up early. Bobbie Lee Taylor was staying at the hotel, and people were crowded on the street outside trying to get in and out the front door. A big Bobbie Lee Taylor sign was up on the hotel. I heard he was in the fifteen-dollar-a-day room, which was up on the third floor, the top floor of the hotel. They could only rent it when a rich person came through town, like the state senator and the manager of the war plant.

After we finished dinner, we went and sat on the porch. It was nice weather for March, and it seemed like an almost summer night had set in. Down in the valley you didn't get the winds, but up in the hills you knew when March came. That was when the pines whistled in the nice sunny weather and the clay got dry and blew up in tan clouds across the cinders until you'd never know they were there. But when April came and the clay washed down you knew the cinders were there and you were glad to have them so you could walk without sinking over your shoes.

Tonight there were big lights over by the schoolhouse where the tent was. It was the first night, and that meant that almost everyone was going to be there. After a year without one, the people in the valley were hungry for a revival. Cars were moving down Main Street bumper to bumper all the way to the foot of it. I could see the red taillights turning into the schoolyard and stopping and going out. Groups of town people were walking down the streets that led to the tent, stopping to pick up other groups standing under street-lights, and getting larger and larger at every corner the closer they got to the foot of Main. The people from out of the hills were there. You could tell by all the trucks covered with hardened clay that were trying to park along the streets. I thought of how many of those trucks were being driven by women, with most of the men overseas. They drove them pretty well, too, and it made me think of how people can sometimes do things you never would have thought they could.

After a while no more cars and trucks came, and only a few people were walking on the streets. I had never seen the town look so full before, with cars and trucks parked on almost every street except the one to the north where the rich people lived. When they wanted they just put a chain across the street and kept traffic out. It was so quiet in town and in the hills that we could hear the singing from the tent, loud and fast. If you didn't know the song, you couldn't understand what they were saying, but I had heard it before.

> "Jesus is my Savior,
> Jesus is my guide,
> Jesus is my guardian,
> Always by my side.
> I'll pray, Jesus, pray, Jesus, pray, Jesus, pray.
> Oh, Lord, I'll pray, Jesus, pray, Jesus, pray, Jesus, pray."

They repeated this last part over and over, faster every time. When the song was done, everything was quiet again, and I looked over to the preacher's. I wondered how he was doing, because it looked like the whole town went to hear Bobbie Lee Taylor. You couldn't tell anything with all the cars parked all over. The ones near his church might be for him or the revival. But they were mostly trucks, and I knew no one was going to come out of the hills, or maybe even from the county seat, just to go to a Bible conference.

Aunt Mae and Mother were talking quietly behind me about Aunt Mae's job in the war plant. Mother asked all the questions, and Aunt Mae was answering about what she was doing and how she was a supervisor now and what good pay she was getting. Mother would say, "Really? Isn't that fine, Mae," and things like that. She was proud of Aunt Mae, and Aunt Mae was too, I think.

Then they started talking about Poppa. Mother said the last letter came from somewhere in Italy. I heard Aunt Mae's rocker just creak for a while, and they were both quiet. Then Aunt Mae said, "That's where the worst fighting is going on, isn't it?" Mother didn't answer, and Aunt Mae rocked slower than she did before.

Bobbie Lee Taylor had been in town for about ten days when Mother decided to go hear him. Aunt Mae said she was tired from the plant and wanted to go to sleep, but Mother was afraid to go down off the hills at night with just me. Finally Aunt Mae said yes, she'd go, so after dinner we all left.

It was April now, but there wasn't any rain yet. The March winds were still in, sweeping out the hills and combing through the pines. The night wasn't bright, because there'd been clouds off and on in the sky during the day and they were staying around for night too. They didn't have enough to start a rain, though. It seemed they could never get together to form one large cloud to do anything.

People were still going to hear Bobbie Lee Taylor, and there were plenty walking down Main Street tonight. Mother didn't know very many people anymore, but Aunt Mae and I did. I saw some of the boys and girls I knew from school and said hello to them, and people said hello to Aunt Mae and nodded at her. They were mostly young and middle-aged, and a few old women from the plant who worked under her.

All along the street trucks were parking in the gutter with women and little children getting out. By the time we got near the foot of Main I was feeling good. I had wanted to come see Bobbie Lee Taylor, but Mother and Aunt Mae waited a long time to make up their minds. Except for the movies, it was one of the few times I got out and went anywhere. Seeing all the people made Mother and Aunt Mae feel good too, and I heard them talking and laughing behind me. We stopped a lot along the way because Mother hadn't been in town for a long time, so she wanted to see what was in the windows.

Outside the tent people were talking in groups, and there was a man selling pop from a stand in the schoolyard. The children who had been in school all day were looking in the schoolhouse windows. I thought that was silly, but then I began to wonder what my room looked like at night, so I went over and looked in and could see the desks from the light of the tent and the rest of the room looking so quiet like you never would imagine a schoolroom could look. Even some of the big boys and girls from Mr. Farney's class looked through the windows to see what his room looked like, and they were telling each other it looked haunted.

We three went into the tent and got a seat up front. The chairs and sawdust made it smell like the lumber company in the county seat. On top of every pole holding up the tent they had strong lights that made it look bright as day in there. About six rows in front of us was the platform. They had big white flowers along the side and on top of the piano.

To the front of it was the kind of stand speechmakers use to put their papers on, except this one had a big black book on it that must have been a Bible.

It got close to seven-thirty, and the people began to come inside. They were still talking in groups when they sat down. The seats began to fill up around us. I saw one or two men, but they were old and held grandchildren on their knees. When I turned around to look, the whole tent was filled, and then Aunt Mae hit me with her elbow. A man was coming onto the platform with a nice suit on. A woman followed him and sat down at the piano. He must have been the man who led the singing. I knew this when he said for us to open tonight with "a good rousing chorus" of some song I never heard of.

> "Sinners can be saints if they'll just bear the cross,
> Sinners can be saints if they'll just bear the cross,
> Sinners can be saints if they'll just bear the cross,
> Bear it and reserve your place in heaven.
> Bear, bear that cross, bear, bear that cross,
> Bear, bear that cross, bear, bear that cross for
>    Jesus."

The man led it loud and the people sang it loud too. He saw they wanted to sing it again, so the woman played the first few bars and everybody sang again. It was an easy song to learn, and I sang it with them the second time. It had a good beat that you could put almost any words to. The woman played it faster the second time, and when it was finished everybody was out of breath and holding on to people they knew and smiling.

Up on the platform the man smiled and held up his hands for everybody to sit down and get quiet. It took a while for people to stop squeaking their chairs, so he waited. When he began to talk again, his face changed and got sad.

"It has been wonderful to be in this town with Bobbie Lee, my friends. So many of you have invited us into your homes to share your humble repasts. God bless all of you, my friends. May the heavens shine down upon you, Christians and sinners alike, for I find it hard to make any distinction. You are all my brothers.

"By now there is no need for me to introduce Bobbie Lee to you all. He has become your friend, your idol, through his own acts. It took no talking on my part to make you love him. Everyone loves a dedicated Christian. Sinners respect one. I hope that by now there is more a feeling of love than respect for this chosen boy. My friends, I may honestly say that I wholeheartedly believe this has come about. But enough from me. Here is *your* Bobbie Lee."

The middle-aged man went over to the side of the platform and coughed and sat down by the piano. We had to wait a few seconds for Bobbie Lee to come on. Everybody was silent, waiting. They looked straight ahead to the platform.

When he came out you could hear people saying to each other, "Oh, here he is," "Bobbie Lee," "Yes, from Memphis," "Shh, listen." I thought Bobbie Lee would be a boy like they said, but he looked about twenty-five to me. I wondered why he wasn't in the war, being of age. His clothes hung on him because he was pretty skinny. But they were good clothes, a good sport coat and different-colored pants with a wide tie that I could count almost six colors on.

The first thing I noticed about him, even before his clothes and how skinny he was, were his eyes. They were blue, but a kind of blue I never saw before. It was a clear kind of eye that always looked like it was staring into a bright light without having to squint. His cheeks weren't full like a boy's would be, but hung in toward his teeth. You could hardly see his upper lip, not because it was thin, but because he had a long, narrow nose that sort of hung down at the end. He was blond-headed, with his hair combed straight back and hanging on his neck.

For a minute he didn't say anything, but opened his Bible and tried to find a page. When he found it he coughed and then looked at the people for another minute. It made everyone uneasy around me. You could hear the wooden chairs squeaking where people were moving. After he ran his eyes over the crowd again, he cleared his throat and spoke in a voice that sounded far away but was still loud.

"Here we are gathered together again for another glorious night of conversion and salvation. I was praying right before I came up here that the testimonies would be many. I was praying that more lost souls would give themselves up to the glory of *Jee*-sus Christ. I feel in my soul that these prayers will be answered, that sinners will surrender to Him by the hundredfold. He don't care who you are. He don't care if you're rich or poor. He don't care if you're babe or grandfather. He just cares if you've got a soul to give Him. That's all *Jee*-sus cares about. Take it from me, my friends, that is all. What more could He want? He don't want worldly riches. They lead to lust. He wants for nothing. He owns a universe. How much do you all own? A car that you use to kill with when you drive under the influence of wine? A house that may easily be turned into a house of sin? A business from which you get worldly riches that lead to sin?

"Today our nation is having a mortal struggle with the devil. In camps young girls are dancing with sailors and soldiers, and who knows what-all. At U.S.O. centers in our cities girls are giving themselves up to the oldest profession before our very eyes. The president's own wife takes a part in these activities. When they're dancing, do you think they're thinking of *Jee*-sus? You can bet your life they aren't. I tried that once. I was dancing with a girl once, and I said to her, 'Are you thinking of *Jee*-sus?' and she pushed me away. She don't realize the importance when she pushed me away. She made me realize that I was representing *Jee*-sus and that *Jee*-sus has no place on the dance floor. No, sir, that is the playground of the devil.

"We have another great menace on our doorsteps. Our men and boys have flown to the other side of the ocean. Are they living with *Jee*-sus over there? Is He in the trenches with them? Are they leading clean Christian lives? They are lost in lands where evil rulers are our enemies. They live in a world of carnage and bloodshed that makes *Jee*-sus Christ weep tears of remorse that He ever peopled this earth. I do not say it is not necessary. It is very necessary, but what type of men will come back to their homes? What type of men will be sitting by the fire, supporting your family, marrying you? They may not even remember the name of *Jee*-sus. Are you prepared for this, or are you fighting it with letters right now that carry the name of *Jee*-sus, that fill your fathers and husbands with new dedication to Him? Ah, the women of America are failing. Every day more soldiers and sailors and marines and colonels and privates and lieutenants are taking up with foreign women and even marrying them! Do you want your son to return home with a foreign wife, maybe even a heathen? That is the cross you women must bear because you have been asleep to the words of *Jee*-sus. Do you want a Chinese in your house taking care of your grand-children, nursing them from her breast? The sins of your men may be your burdens in the future. Think of this before you write him your next letter. Include the glorious words of the Bible, of Matthew, of Genesis.

"Now I may ask *you* a question. What about *you*? Are you being faithful to the men while they are away? It is a great chance to be free and do as you please, isn't it? Nowadays you can see women all over in the factories, driving buses in the cities. They may go where they want, dance and honky-tonk at the army bases, ride the trains and highways without a restraining hand. The devil is tempting these women, drawing them into his web. Are you fighting the devil, or are you falling under his influence?"

Somewhere in the back a woman began to cry, and people started turning around to see who it was, but remembered they shouldn't. When the chairs stopped squeaking, he went on.

"Ah, we have heard a voice, a voice in the wilderness. She don't fear *Jee*-sus, she wants His compassion. How many of you other women are stifling tears of repentance? Don't be afraid. Let *Jee*-sus know you're sorry. Cry to Him for mercy."

The woman next to me began crying, and so did a lot of other women too. She was about sixty-five years old, and I knew she couldn't have done anything wrong.

"*Jee*-sus hears those tears of remorse. He is rejoicing in His kingdom. True repentance is the only thing, friends, the only thing. Let us pour forth our hearts to Him. Then we will see the light, then we will get the true feeling."

In the front row a woman screamed, "Oh, Lord," and fell on her knees on the sawdust. Bobbie Lee Taylor was beginning to sweat. It was getting hot in the tent, and though I knew nobody was smoking, the air looked like they were. From the back somewhere somebody else screamed, but I couldn't make out what they said. It started up high and loud and ended in a sort of a moan. All down my row the people's eyes were shining. There was just one old woman who held her head in her hands. She was crying.

"Oh, isn't this glorious, friends. Tears for the Lord. He don't care what you were. He just wants a new soul for his flock. I prayed that tonight we'd see glorious conversions. How my prayers are coming true, friends, how they are coming true! *Jee*-sus is with us tonight. He feels that a band of dedicated people are asking for a new birth. He is ready to accept His new sheep into the fold.

"Now, while we sing 'Rock of Ages,' I want every one of you who has felt a new birth in their soul to come up here on the platform. *Jee*-sus don't give a hoot what your past life was. He is willing to forgive and forget. He will welcome you with open arms. He wants you. Try living with *Jee*-sus and see how glorious your life can be. What a band of crusaders you will be, my friends, those of you who are willing to testify to Him that you will fight the Christian battle. We don't want cowards to testify tonight, we want only dedicated Christians. Come up and be born again, my friends. Let us bow our heads and sing."

The piano player struck up the tune, and everybody started singing. I looked at Bobbie Lee. His mouth was tight, and he was breathing hard.

"'Rock of ages, cleft for me . . .'"

I heard some footsteps in the sawdust. I heard Bobbie Lee.

"They're coming, they're coming out of the rows and up the aisle. Why don't you join them, my friends. Why don't you unburden your strayed hearts."

I felt the woman next to me get up. Chairs were squeaking all over the tent.

"'Let me hide myself in thee . . .'"

"Oh, isn't this a glorious night for Him! What a defeat for the devil, friends. I can see them coming, young and old. I can see the look of dedication in their eyes. Oh, why don't you join them. Won't it be wonderful if we have a great crowd up here as a grand testimony to Him?"

There were more chairs squeaking and footsteps in the aisle. Some of them were crying as they went by.

"Let's take another chorus, friends. Some of you have not made your decisions yet. Don't pass up this opportunity. Make up your minds while we sing it again."

The piano player struck up again, and everybody sang quieter and slower. There were some more footsteps, but not as many as before.

When we finished the chorus Bobbie Lee said, "Here they are. They want to dedicate themselves to *Jee*-sus. We'll let a few of them speak. Oh, what a glorious turn their lives have taken tonight."

There were quite a few people on the platform. Most of them were women, but they had some of the big boys from Mr. Farney's room up there changing from one foot to the other. All in all I'd say there must have been about fifty of them.

Bobbie Lee took a woman by the arm and brought her up

to the microphone. She was biting her lip she was so scared. He asked her for her testimony.

"I'm Mrs. Ollie Ray Wingate, and I live here in town." She stopped to clear her throat and think of what to say. "For a long time now . . . for a long time now I've been feeling that I needed the help of Jesus. So many of my friends came here and told me about it. I'm glad that I had the courage to testify and . . . and I hope you all who have not come up yet will come up before Bobbie Lee leaves town."

She started to cry, and Bobbie Lee helped her away from the microphone.

"Weren't those words of inspiration? Let's hear from this lady."

The old woman who had been sitting next to me came up and spoke.

"Most of you know me. I own the grocery on Main. But friends and neighbors, let me tell you I never felt this way before. I am resigned to the Lord to judge me and forget my past sins. I want to repent and be converted to His way." Tears started to roll down her cheeks again. "I want to walk in the Garden of Eden with Him. Our Bobbie Lee has put a new meaning in my life. My soul feels like it never felt before. It took Bobbie Lee to get the name of Rachel Carter on the rolls of converts. For fifty years I wanted to come up and testify, but no one gave me the strength until now when this dedicated young man showed up."

Bobbie Lee helped her away.

"Thank you, Mrs. Carter, for opening your heart to us and showing us what it feels like to have the light beaming in. You see, friends, she don't have to fear that she can stand up to any Christian now."

The next one up was a boy from Mr. Farney's class. He looked at the microphone and swallowed hard. Bobbie Lee said, "Don't be afraid of *Jee*-sus, boy."

"My name is Billy Sunday Thompson, and I go to school here in the eighth grade. Er, I just want to say that I am glad to dedicate myself to Jesus and I'm glad I finally came up because I felt I needed Jesus for a long time."

He put his head down and stepped back.

"Friends, those were the words of a babe, while many of you grandfathers here are afraid to come up. That testimony should inspire you grandfathers and grandmothers who will not come up. Wouldn't you all feel good if you would have testified at this age. The Lord may take you any time, yet you are not preparing for that great day."

Some of the others testified, and a few just looked like they didn't know what to do up on the platform. The little children whose mothers went up were beginning to cry for them, so Bobbie Lee knew the testimonies would have to stop. He gave the piano player a signal and said for us not to forget the donation box in the back of the tent, which was the only support for this revival, and that he would be back tomorrow night with another message that nobody would want to miss, and if they couldn't catch him tomorrow night, and he hoped they could, he would still be in town through Monday.

The piano player started to play some fast song, and Bobbie Lee and the people on the platform went out through a little opening at the back of the tent. As they were disappearing, the people in the audience started to leave too. They stopped and talked with each other at the ends of rows and in the aisles, so it took a while for Aunt Mae and I

and Mother to get out. By the time we got to the outside, the
piano player had stopped, and the man who led the songs,
the middle-aged one, was taking the white flowers off the
platform.

Outside it was a lot cooler. I took a deep breath. All over in
the schoolyard and in the street people were talking and
drinking pop they bought from the man with the stand. We
began walking home, but some woman who knew Aunt Mae
from the plant stopped and talked to us. She was going our
way down Main, so she walked with us.

Along the curb children and women were getting into the
cars and trucks, and they were starting up, and their lights
were going on. People walked in the street and jumped out
of the way to let trucks pass them. Sometimes children just
stood in front of the trucks with their arms out and pretended they wouldn't let them pass, but just when the trucks
got near them, they laughed and ran away. I wished I was
one of those children who could ride in the back of the
trucks and hang my feet over the tailgate and feel the wind
rushing all around me. The only bad time to ride there was
when it rained.

The woman talking to Aunt Mae was the kind that talked
a lot. For a while she talked about the plant and how she
never thought she would ever be working at her age, and in a
plant, too, which was a man's work. She said her son was on
an island somewhere in the Pacific Ocean, and he wrote her
and told her how proud he was she worked in a war plant.
With her son's money and what she was making, she never
saw so much money before in her life, but she worried about
what Bobbie Lee said. She said her next letter to her son
would have something in it about Bobbie Lee, he was such a

wonderful man, one of God's chosen, and her son should know what he said about the boys overseas so he wouldn't make any mistakes, because she told Aunt Mae she didn't want any Chinee grandbabies on her knee with their dangerous-looking mother hanging around the house. She asked me if I liked Bobbie Lee, and I said yes, I thought he was pretty good being able to speak like that for so long without ever stopping or forgetting something like we did at school. She had gone up the second night he was in town. She went up every time the evangelists came to town because she said you can never get too much of that. She wanted to know why none of us went up, so Aunt Mae told her that we hadn't made our minds up yet. We'd better do it quick, she said, because Bobbie Lee was going to be here only a few more nights, and you might as well be in God's favor with all they said about Hitler sending a bomb over.

We left her at some street near the beginning of the hills. When she was gone Aunt Mae said something to Mother about her that I didn't hear. By the time we were halfway up the hill to the house, all the lights were off over at the tent and the last trucks were starting and lighting up and going off. I saw Bobbie Lee next when he was leaving town and Miss Moore took us on a field trip to see him off.

# Five

With a lot of women who had never worked before having jobs in the war plant and getting money from their husbands in the war, most people had more money in our valley than they ever did have. They didn't have too much to spend it on with the ration books for almost everything. In the grocery you could see everybody looking in their books trying to figure out which coupon to use for what. Nobody seemed to have enough, especially people with a big family. Aunt Mae and Mother and I always didn't have meat or butter or something because there weren't any more coupons for them.

We got oleomargarine for the first time, too. When I first saw it, I thought it was lard. Mother brought the box into the kitchen and put it in a bowl and dropped a red bean in and started to mix it. It was thick and hard to mix. After a while the bean disappeared and the lard started to get yellow. By the time it was creamy it looked like butter. I didn't mind the taste. I kind of liked it, though it was salty at first. That night we just had bread toasted in the oven with oleo, and cabbage with some pickle meat, because Aunt Mae used the coupons we needed to get good meat to get something else. The ration book made Mother go down into town more than she did before. She was the only one who knew how to use it.

One night that summer the women at the plant had a party. Aunt Mae was a chairman of it because of her job. The whole day she spent down at the plant decorating and helping them with the food. When she got home, she went right up to her room to get ready. I was going with Mother and Aunt Mae, and I wanted to see what it would be like because I didn't go to a party since I started school.

At about seven o'clock Mother and I were ready sitting on the porch waiting for Aunt Mae. Mother had on a good dress, and I was wearing my suit, a nice gabardine one. It was a wonderful night for a party, warm and clear, with just a little warm breeze. I hoped they had punch and sandwiches with the crusts cut off. We didn't eat any dinner because we were going to get food there.

After a while Aunt Mae came out, and she really looked good. She was wearing a dress she bought in town. It was maroon crepe with silver glitter around the neck. In the shoulders they had big pads that made Aunt Mae look strong, and the skirt just came to her knees. I liked her shoes because I never saw a pair like them before, with the toes sticking out and a little strap around her ankle. I thought what nice legs Aunt Mae had. Mother got out a handkerchief and wiped some of the red off Aunt Mae's cheeks, and Aunt Mae fussed about it. When Mother finished, she got out the little powder box she had in her purse and looked at herself in the mirror in it.

All the way down the path to town Aunt Mae told us to go slower because of her shoes. It smelled good on the path. Not only because of Aunt Mae, but because the summer flowers were out and the honeysuckle was climbing along the old stumps. Even though it was seven-thirty, the night hadn't set in yet. It was more like twilight, and the hills always looked pretty then.

Down in town a lot of people were walking over to the river where the plant was. When we got there, there were plenty trucks parked along the river and in the plant parking lot. Almost all the women getting out were dressed up with flowers in their hair. It must have been the honeysuckle from the hills, because you could smell it all over and I knew it didn't grow down by the river.

We went into the big room in the plant where they put the parts together. The small machines were pushed up against the wall, and that left a big space on the floor for dancing. There weren't too many dances in the valley. Now with the war on and the men gone there hadn't been one in a long time. Aunt Mae went behind a table where they had some food and helped the women there. Mother and I just sat on a chair by a big gray machine and watched the people.

A band came after we were there about fifteen minutes. It had a piano, a bass fiddle, a banjo, and a trumpet. The players were from the county seat, I think, and were all men except for the woman who played the piano. They struck up a lively tune that I'd heard plenty times before but didn't know the name. A few women started dancing with each other. Except for Aunt Mae, they all had on thin summer dresses with flower patterns all over. You could see the flowers moving across the floor, a rose pattern with a gardenia and a violet with a sunflower.

The room was pretty filled. More people came in all the time and stood around against the tin walls and the machines. Some would start in dancing with each other, or see someone they knew and start talking. Before we knew it, Aunt Mae was on the floor dancing with that woman who walked home with us after the night we saw Bobbie Lee. Aunt Mae took the man's part, and she was swinging the woman all over. The band was playing a song I always heard on the radio called "Chattanooga Choo Choo." When they saw what Aunt Mae and the woman were doing, the other dancers moved back in a circle and let them have the whole floor. Mother and I stood up on our chairs to see over the heads of all the people who had crowded around the floor. They were calling, "Look at Flora"—which was the name of the other woman—and "Swing her, Miss Gebler," and "Look at those two go."

When it was over everyone clapped. Aunt Mae got through the crowd of women who were patting her on the back and came over and sat down by us. She was trying to fix a heel on her shoe that came loose. It wouldn't go back on, so Aunt Mae sat by Mother and they talked. By now the floor was full of women dancing and trying to watch out for the little children who ran in and out between them. Aunt Mae watched them, and I knew she was disappointed over the heel.

The women walking past where we sat were carrying big glasses full of white foam that dripped over the sides. They didn't usually have beer at any party in town, and Aunt Mae said the manager of the factory sent it over from the capital, where they had the brewery. She told me to go get her a glass. I could hardly get through to the table where they were giving it out, there were so many women and little children around it. Aunt Mae took her glass and took a long drink, then got a faraway look in her eye and belched.

It was almost ten o'clock. Most of the beer was gone, but there were still plenty dancers on the floor. The little children were sleeping on top of the machines with their legs hanging down the sides. Women stopped by where we were sitting and told Aunt Mae it was the best party they'd been to since they were girls. After a while the band played a waltz, and Mother asked me if I wanted to dance. I never danced before, but we didn't do too bad. Mother was a good dancer, though, so she took the boy's part. I was almost as tall as she was, so I don't know how we looked.

Some woman got up where the band was playing and asked if there was anybody who could sing. Nobody in town sang except the woman at the preacher's church, but she had the kind of high voice that nobody liked. Flora, the woman who danced with Aunt Mae, got up by the band with the other woman and said that Miss Gebler, the supervisor, told her she used to sing. Everybody looked over where we were sitting. Aunt Mae said no, she hadn't sung in years, and she'd just make them hate her, but everybody told her to come on or they wouldn't go home that night. After they went on this way for a while Aunt Mae said alright, like I knew she wanted to say when they first asked her. Aunt Mae had a few beers, so I wondered what she'd do. She took off her shoes, because of the heel, and went on up to the band and talked with them for about a minute.

Then the piano started up and played a few notes. Aunt Mae nodded her head. The big fiddle began to thump, and the piano started again with the banjo. Aunt Mae turned around.

"Saint Louis woman with your diamond rings
Got this man of mine by your apron strings . . ."

The trumpet blew a few notes here that sounded real good. Aunt Mae sounded good too. I didn't know she sang like this. Her voice was better than any I ever heard outside of the movies. I looked at Mother, and she was looking at Aunt Mae with her eyes all watery. The women stared at her. Nobody in the valley heard anyone ever sing a song like that except on the radio.

Aunt Mae finished, and they all whistled and clapped. They wanted her to sing again, but the only song the band knew that she knew was "God Bless America," so she sang it. It was a song that you always heard on the radio then, and everybody sang it with her the second time. When that was over, the women all grabbed ahold of Aunt Mae and hugged her. She was crying as she came to where we were.

As we walked home up the path, the cool summer night had set in. No matter how hot it was in the day, it was cool in the hills at night. Aunt Mae had talked all the way home after we left the plant, after everyone had stopped talking to her and we got away at last. We left after midnight and were the last ones to go except for the night watchman. It was about one now. Up ahead I could see the house with the lights on. I could feel my bed under me, but Aunt Mae was going slow. Right when we got into the yard and could hear the cinders grinding under our feet, Aunt Mae turned

around and looked down at the town and held Mother by
the arm.

"You know, I never thought I'd be happy here."

Then she looked out onto the hills and the night sky.

We didn't see much of Aunt Mae after that. One of the old
men who played in the band at the plant that night asked her
if she wanted to sing with them all the time. They had a lot
of jobs in the hills playing and went into the county seat and
the capital sometimes, too. When Aunt Mae came home
from the plant in the evening, she put on the dress she wore
to sing with the band and went off. The old man met her at
the foot of the hill in his truck with the bass fiddle in the
back. I used to sit on the porch in the twilight when the night
birds were beginning to sing and watch Aunt Mae go down
the path in her good dress and disappear where the hill got
steep and I couldn't see her anymore. A while later I could
see the old man's truck going off down Main Street with
Aunt Mae's arm resting on the door and the big fiddle in the
back.

The newspaper had a story in it about the band once, with
a picture of Aunt Mae singing along. It was like all the other
pictures in our paper. Aunt Mae's hair looked like a cloud
with a bunch of colored men playing behind her. In all the
pictures people's skin was always dark and their hair white,
no matter what color it really was. The story told all about
how Aunt Mae was once a famous singer and that people like
her were needed in the valley to make people feel good. Mr.
Watkins wrote a letter to the editor about the story. It said

that the people of the valley needed a lot more things before they needed Aunt Mae. Then Aunt Mae wrote a letter that said the valley needed a lot less people like Mr. Watkins, if it needed anything. They didn't have any more letters in the paper on either side, and I thought it was over when the preacher got into it.

He put an ad in the paper that had a list of reasons from the Bible why the band and Aunt Mae weren't doing anyone any good. After Bobbie Lee Taylor left, the town was split over the preacher. The people who didn't go to the preacher's conference when Bobbie Lee was in town were dropped from the church rolls. The people who got dropped were mad at the preacher because everyone liked to go to church if he could pay the pledge. Of course, there were people like us who didn't belong to the church when all this happened, and the preacher said they were the kind that "didn't care which way the wind blew."

The people who were dropped bought an ad in the paper the next day and gave a list of reasons why Aunt Mae and the band were good for the valley. It started that on Saturday night the moviehouse began to have Aunt Mae and the band besides the movie for ten cents more. The second Saturday that they were there some people who belonged to the church walked up and down in front of the moviehouse with big signs about the evil inside. When the editor of the paper heard about this, he got a picture of them on the front page. Our paper went all the way into the county seat, and even plenty people in the capital bought it. They saw the picture of the people with the signs and, like people always do, came to see Aunt Mae the next Saturday night. That night the town looked almost like Bobbie Lee was there. Trucks were parked all over, and only a few out of all those people could get into the moviehouse. You couldn't even find the preacher's people with the signs in the crowd on Main Street. The people came back the next Saturday night who couldn't get in, and by then the sheriff told the preacher his people were creating a nuisance and would be removed. They had done his brother's business all the good they could.

After this the preacher sort of set himself off from the town. Mr. and Mrs. Watkins and the others who were still on the rolls tried to fight anything the town did, and even sent a few of themselves to the state legislature to see about the moviehouse. This didn't get anywhere because the governor was a friend of the sheriff, but it did make the preacher's people get even closer together, and there were quite a few of them. They bought time on the town's radio station for the preacher to speak on Sunday night at the time *Amos 'n' Andy* came on. The people who didn't belong anymore, and those who didn't in the first place, got mad because *Amos 'n' Andy* was everybody's favorite. The only other station you could get was the one strong one in the capital, but it never came in well.

Meanwhile Aunt Mae was going with the old man and the fiddle in the truck every night. They got famous all over our part of the state. When the soldiers came home on furloughs, they got married to the girls they'd been writing letters to in town. A lot of girls who never expected to get married were asked to by soldiers they knew since school who were home for two weeks. Aunt Mae and the band got plenty business from all the wedding receptions going on in our section. People didn't usually dance at wedding receptions like they did in the movies. If the preacher married you, you couldn't do it, but people liked to sit around and listen to the band and Aunt Mae. Mother and I went to a lot of receptions that way that we never would have been invited to. Mother told me Aunt Mae didn't get half the money she should for singing with the band, but I knew she liked to do it and would sing even if they didn't pay her anything, most likely.

Mother was worried about the letters she got from Poppa. He was right in the middle of the fighting in Italy. In one letter he said he was living in an old farmhouse that was about a thousand years old. He wrote about the olive trees, and that made me think, because I always saw olives in a bottle, whole or with the red stuff in the middle, but I never thought they grew anywhere. He said he had marched along the Appian Way, too, which was a very famous road that I'd read about in history and would be able to tell my teacher about. The sun wasn't prettier anywhere else, he said, than it was in Italy. It was the brightest and yellowest he ever saw, much brighter than in the valley in the middle of the summer. He saw where the pope lived, too, and I had heard about him plenty times when the preacher was talking over the radio in place of *Amos 'n' Andy*, who I liked. The beaches were nice there too, he said. When he returned he was going to take me to the ocean, because I never went there, so I could see what a beach was like with the waves rolling up it. In the end he said he missed every one of us more than he ever thought he would.

All his letters Mother kept in a tin box in the kitchen over the icebox. Aunt Mae read them all twice or more, especially the ones where he described how pretty Italy was. Aunt Mae said she always wanted to go there and see Rome and Milan and Florence and the Tiber River. One letter Poppa sent had some photographs of some Italian people in it. They looked healthy, and even the old woman in the picture was carrying a big bundle. Poppa was standing between two Italian girls in one picture. None of the girls in the valley had thick black hair like they did. Mother smiled when she saw the picture, and I did too. Poppa was so serious it was funny to see him standing smiling with his arms around two girls. Aunt Mae laughed when she saw it and said, "My, he must have changed."

Down in school I was doing alright in Miss Moore's. It was my last year with her. In spring I would get out of sixth and go into Mr. Farney's. With Miss Moore we went all over on field trips. After we finished going all through the valley, we went to the county seat and saw the courthouse. The school didn't have a bus because it was easy for everybody to get to who lived in the valley. It would have been harder to get a bus into the hills than to have everybody just walk there. For our trip to the county seat Miss Moore got the state to send a bus to the school. Everybody went "pew" when they got inside, because it smelled bad. I thought I knew the smell from somewhere before, and I thought for a while, and then I remembered Mrs. Watkins' breath. It smelled just like that.

I always thought Miss Moore was a little deaf. I know some other people thought it too, but I never said anything to anybody about it because there was always some way that stories got back to her. When we got in the bus and everybody went "pew," Miss Moore didn't say anything. She sat down on the front seat and started wiggling her nose. She asked the driver if he could open the windows, and he said that they were sealed because some children tried to jump out once while the bus was moving. I never felt a bus shake you up and down so much as that one did. Even when it hit the smallest bumps it made everybody go "uh." Miss Moore made us start singing some song we knew from school. Because of the bus the long notes always sounded like "uh-uh-uh-uh-uh-uh-uh" and never straight like they should be. Some of the bad boys who were sitting in the back started singing other words that they made up. For about the past year I understood what they were singing about. Miss Moore didn't hear them, though, and when we stopped she said, "That was nice."

But the singing started the bad boys, so they began to tell jokes and recite poems that no one said out loud. None of the girls laughed because it wasn't nice for them to do it, and any girl who did was pretty bad. There was one girl, though, named Eva, who didn't laugh but just giggled. The other girls looked at her and probably told their mothers when they got home. Up front the driver was laughing at what they said. Miss Moore smiled at him. She probably thought it was nice for an old man to have such a happy disposition. I didn't know what to think about the bad boys. Some of the things they said were pretty funny, but I didn't know if I should laugh, so I just looked straight ahead like the girls and pretended I didn't hear them. They started saying things about Miss Moore I didn't believe. Even if she wasn't too smart, she was still a nice woman.

At the courthouse there was a statue of a naked woman holding a big vase. The bad boys stood around it in a circle and laughed and pointed at things. Miss Moore and the rest of us didn't even look at it when we passed, but I got a pretty good idea of what it looked like out the corner of my eye.

Miss Moore wouldn't go back and get the boys, so some man who worked at the courthouse told them to move on. There wasn't much to see there, though, besides the statue. We sat in the courtroom and listened to a judge talk to some colored man about taking somebody's mule. Then there was a man who was drunk, and that was all.

We sat out on the grass in front of the courthouse and ate the sandwiches we brought, and Miss Moore asked us how we liked it, and we said it was okay. The courthouse was a real old building. At the top it had colored glass windows in one place instead of a roof. All the time we ate, the bad boys were up in the windows making signs. Miss Moore couldn't see them because she was sitting with her back to the courthouse. If she had turned around and seen them up there she probably would have put them out of school. Everybody knew what those signs meant, and the girls looked down at the grass and pretended to be looking for clovers. Miss Moore saw them doing this and started looking for clovers herself. After a while I saw a man come up behind the boys in the window and pull them away. About a week after we came back from that trip, the judge at the county seat wrote Miss Moore a letter that she read to us about how bad we were at the courthouse. Miss Moore didn't know what he was talking about, and she got mad and wrote him back a letter that we all helped her write, especially the bad boys, that said the judge must have had the wrong school on his mind.

When spring came I was almost out of sixth grade. We were going to have a play at the end of school that Miss Moore wrote. The day we started practicing for it, we didn't get out of school until five o'clock. It was a nice spring afternoon, just like all the ones we had in the valley. In town everybody's garden was full of flowers. The grass in the yards was green and full of dandelions. The warm breeze that always smelled a little like the pines in the hills was blowing through the streets.

In the spring the prettiest place in the valley was the hills. Up along the path all the wildflowers were beginning to come out. If there was snow that winter, the ground would be damp and warm. We did have a lot of snow that year that made it hard to get down the path to school, but now the only thing that would tell you it had been there was the wet mud. All the pines looked greener than they had for a long time. The warm air smelled strong of them, much stronger than in town. All the birds were back too, and they sang and flew from pine to pine and dropped down to the ground and flew back up again. Sometimes I would see a broken egg along the path that fell from a nest up in the pines, and I thought what a fine bird it might have been. Sometimes a little baby bird would fall out too, and I saw it there dead and blue. I didn't like to see dead animals. I never hunted like plenty people in the valley did. Some just shot at a bird to test their aim.

Spring was really the time I was glad we lived in the hills. Everything was moving. The breeze made the pines sway, and the little animals played in the grass and the low bushes. Sometimes a rabbit would run across the cinders in our front yard. Everything was moving that evening I was walking home. It made you feel you weren't alone on the path. Every step I made, something would move. Down in the wet mud I could see the holes that the worms made and the bigger holes of some bugs. I wondered what it would be like to live down in the wet mud with the water going by you every time

it rained and your home liable to be knocked in when someone stepped on it, or else be trapped when someone just
closed the opening and you couldn't get out. I wondered
what happened to bugs that were just trapped and if they
starved to death. I wondered what it would be like to starve
to death.

Up ahead the house was sitting right in the middle of the
cinders. It looked like it was a part of the hill, just a big box
of wood without any paint on it. It looked brown like the
trunk of a pine, and the mold on the roof was a greenish
color. The only part that made it look like people lived in it
was the white curtains blowing out of Aunt Mae's bedroom
window and the pair of woman's pink underwear hanging
on a clothes hanger from the window shade to dry.

I went in the front door and put my books and my copy of
Miss Moore's play on the stairs. Mother usually sat on the
front porch these spring afternoons because she liked the
pine breeze. I hadn't seen her there, though. Something
began to smell like it was burning, so I went into the kitchen,
and there was a pot on the stove full of smoke and Mother
was sitting on a chair with her head on the table crying. At
first I didn't know if she was crying or what, because she let
out little screams every now and then and scratched her nails
into the oilcloth. I picked up the piece of yellow paper on
the table. It was a telegram. We never got one. I only knew
about them from the movies. No one in the valley got tele-
grams. It was addressed to Mother. It was from the govern-
ment. It said Poppa was dead. Killed in Italy.

I held it in my hand. Poppa was dead? We just got a letter
from him the day before saying he thought the worst of the
fighting was over. I went over to where Mother was sitting

and tried to make her sit up, but she acted like she didn't even feel my hand on her. She kept screaming and scratching the oilcloth. I shook her by the shoulders, but she just screamed louder, so I let her alone and went over to the stove and turned off the fire under the pot.

I went outside to get away from the burning smell in the kitchen. We didn't have any chairs on the back porch, so I sat down on the back steps and looked up into the hills. Aunt Mae was still at the plant. She had a party to sing for tonight that they were giving in the county seat for some soldier home on a furlough. I wondered if she'd go to it. Poppa and Aunt Mae never got along. She didn't have any reason to feel bad.

I looked back at the telegram and thought of how funny it was that a few black letters on some yellow paper could make people feel the way it made Mother feel. I thought what it would do if the black letters were just changed around a little to read something else, anything. I wondered where they had Poppa now so far away from home where he should have died. No one I ever knew well died before. This was the first time, and I didn't know how to feel. I always thought people should cry, but I couldn't. I just sat there and thought about where Poppa was, and if they were going to send his body home like they did some. What was it like to have your father's grave somewhere where you could never visit it like you should or put flowers on it or know he was resting in peace? Then I imagined what Poppa looked like now that he was dead. I only saw one funeral in my life, and the person looked all white. Poppa's skin was red and oily, and I couldn't think of him being white and powdery-looking.

Behind the house I could see the place Poppa tried to

grow some things, the place Mother took care of after he left until the things all came up. That was about a year ago. The ground was wet like all the other ground in the hills, and grass was beginning to grow in it where he had it all cleared and there wasn't any shade from the pines. You could still see the high places where the rows were, but they were beginning to wear down from the snows, and now that the grass was out, everything looked almost even. A few seedling pines were growing up there too, and I knew that when a few more years came and they were tall, the whole little place would look just like any other place in the hills and you'd never know anyone spent almost all of one week's pay on it and put in a lot of time too. You'd never think in a few more years someone almost left his house over that piece of clay and hit his wife in the jaw and scared his son. But besides me, that was the only thing Poppa did while he was living that you could see now. I thought of the letter where he said he was going to take me to see the beach and the waves when he got home, and Poppa's little cleared land got all blurry, and I knew I was crying.

# Six

Then the war was over. The paper had headlines six inches high, and the drugstore gave away free firecrackers that everybody shot off on Main Street. It was summer, and it was hot in the valley. In the summer there wasn't any breeze. It was just still and hot. I sat on the porch and listened to the firecrackers down in town. You could hear them all over the valley, even from the county seat. When night came the whole town lighted up except a few houses where men had been killed, like ours. I could sit there and pick them out. The big gray one on Main Street where the woman's husband was killed in Germany, the small old one where a colored woman lived whose son was killed on some island, one or two clean white ones on the street where the rich people lived, a house on the hill across from us where an old maid's brother was killed who was a bachelor and lived with

93

her, and some others I didn't know about but just saw the dark space in between all the other lights.

That night was just like the day had been, hot and still, even in the hills. I could hear radios playing loud from down in town. Some had the baseball game, but most were listening to the news about the end of the war. Our radio was playing upstairs where Mother and Aunt Mae were listening to it, but it was some waltz music from someplace in New York. Down on the streets people were still going to one another's house or meeting on the street and laughing. The preacher's Bible was on like always. Once in the war we had an air raid practice in the valley and he got into trouble with the sheriff because he wouldn't turn it off. The preacher was probably glad the war was over too. While it was going on, not many people attended, not even the ones who stayed with him after the Bobbie Lee Taylor thing.

The next day everybody's clothesline was full of bed-clothes and shirts for the husbands and brothers and sons who were coming home. By the time Christmas came, plenty were home. They all had babies from the girls they married on their furloughs. Everybody had up a Christmas tree but us and those other houses where the lights weren't on the night the war was over. They still had their service flag in the window where they didn't want to or forgot to take it down. We still had ours on the front door too. None of us wanted to touch it.

By the next spring the seedling pines in Poppa's cleared land were getting tall and beginning to look like real pines. Down in town all the babies were beginning to walk, and there were new ones coming in. When I walked home from Mr. Farney's class in the evening all the girls were out on the front porches where they lived with their parents or their husband's parents, and I could see they were all going to have other babies soon too. Almost all the soldiers were in then. Some of them went off to the college at the capital with their wives and babies, but plenty stayed right in town because they hadn't even been to the high school at the county seat.

Mr. Watkins wrote a letter to the paper that he had never seen so many pregnant women on the streets and that he was disgusted with the sight of them. Then the paper got a lot of letters from the pregnant women asking him what they were supposed to do about it. One woman wrote she was curious to know why Mr. Watkins and his wife never had any children. The next Sunday night Mrs. Watkins got on the preacher's radio program and said she was glad she never had any children to have to bring up in this sinful world alongside of the kind of children that woman would have.

Some of the men came back to the valley with women they married in Europe. The town people wouldn't have anything to do with them, so they all got together and moved to the capital. On the radio the preacher said it was good riddance and that he didn't want to see the good American blood of the valley lose its purity. That won a lot of the town people back to his side, so pretty soon the church rolls were filled again and kept on growing. Some got together in the church hall and organized a society to keep the valley blood pure and Christian and free from the heathen blood that might ruin it and bring damnation to the valley. Not everyone in town joined it, but it had a pretty big membership. It met once a week for a while until all the soldiers who weren't killed got home, and then they didn't need it anymore.

Some of the killed men started coming home too. They delivered them at the station just like mail. About once a month one would come to the valley, but just his people went to get the body. No one thought too much about the dead ones. The living ones were all over with their new babies and families. I don't guess anyone wanted to think about the ones who came to the station in the long wooden boxes. Anyway, no one did, except maybe the newspaper editor, who always had something in the paper about it when one came in. The women who hadn't cried since they heard about their son or brother or husband getting killed cried all over again when the bodies came in at the station. Then they were put in somebody's truck and taken to the graveyard up in the hills. Sometimes I'd see one of those trucks going down Main Street with a woman sitting up front crying and a man driving with the long box bumping in the back. The little children would run away when they saw one coming because it frightened them. After they got out of town, they turned up the north hill to the graveyard. If the woman was on the preacher's rolls, they'd stop at the church to get him to go with them. Then they came down from the hill about an hour later and left the preacher off, and the woman was still crying.

Poppa never did come home. They buried him in Italy somewhere. Mother got a picture of the place. It was nothing but rows and rows of white crosses, and Mother wondered which one was Poppa's. Aunt Mae had to hide the picture from her because she just sat down and looked at it and said, "Maybe this one," and pointed, or "It could be that one, Mae," or she'd ask Aunt Mae which one she thought it was. When she couldn't find the picture, she got mad, so Aunt Mae had to give it back to her. Pretty soon it was all torn and yellow, and the crosses were smeared and greasy from Mother rubbing her finger across it. When Aunt Mae went out to sing at night, I'd sit with Mother and watch her look at the picture. She never even knew I was there, but just sat and felt the picture, and then she'd turn it over and look on the back and laugh when she saw there wasn't anything there. I knew I shouldn't be frightened of my own mother, but I was, and I'd wait for Aunt Mae to come home and hope she'd hurry up.

The war plant closed, so Aunt Mae didn't have her job anymore. The only money she made was at night when the band went out. She tried to get a job down in town, but all the men who returned had all the jobs. The only thing she could do was be a maid for the rich people who lived on the street to the north, and Aunt Mae didn't want a job like that. All the colored girls would call her white trash if she took a job like that, so she stayed around the house while I was away at school and helped Mother, who couldn't seem to do anything anymore. Mother would begin to clean and then go get the picture from her room and sit and look at it, or else she burned the food when she tried to cook and didn't even smell it to take it off the stove. One day Aunt Mae told her to go sit on the porch while she worked in the house. When I got home from school that afternoon, Aunt Mae ran down the path to get me with a wild look in her eyes. I was scared when I saw her coming and didn't know what was wrong. She grabbed me by the shoulders and said she told Mother to go sit on the porch and now she couldn't find her. That strange feeling ran up my legs and stopped, the one I always get when I'm scared. I told Aunt Mae I didn't see her coming up the path. We went back to the house and looked all over, but we couldn't find her. It was getting dark. Mother was nowhere in the house, so I went up into the hills to walk around and try to think where she could be. I walked through the old place that Poppa had cleared. The pines there were a fine size now. The twilight was always pretty in the pines. I stopped and looked around and thought I heard something by the base of one of them. It was Mother digging at the ground. She looked up and saw me and turned back to the pine and smiled.

"Oh, David, aren't your father's cabbages growing big! I never thought his vegetables would get anywhere in all this clay, but just look. Big, big cabbages your poppa grew."

Aunt Mae got up in the mornings now and made my lunch for school. She learned more about cooking by now and didn't do so bad. When I got off she dressed Mother and let her go outside.

In school I was almost out of Mr. Farney's, which meant I was almost out of grade school. Mr. Farney was different from the other people in the valley. I heard he was from Atlanta, but that wasn't why he was different. It was the way he acted that made him strange. He didn't walk like the other men did. He walked more like a woman who swayed her hips. You could always tell Mr. Farney by his walk, no matter what clothes he was wearing and even if his back was turned to you. He had small feet that sort of pointed in when he walked. He had thin black hair that just lay soft on his head like a baby's. The main thing about Mr. Farney that was different when you saw him was his face. I knew he was almost thirty, but his skin was smooth, and you could see thin blue veins in his forehead and his nose and on his hands. His eyes were the clearest blue you ever saw and were big and wide. Everything else about him was thin, his nose, his mouth, and his body. No matter whether it was warm or cold his ears were always red, and you could almost see through them in some places.

If he wasn't so smart the boys in our class would have laughed at him. They talked about him all the time, but they never did anything in class. He could recite anything in the line of a poem or something from a famous book, and no one else in town even read poems or many books. Sometimes he wrote poems himself. The editor of the paper would print them, but nobody knew what they meant. Oh, some people who thought they were smart said they did, but I knew they didn't. His poems didn't rhyme like everybody thought they should, so Mr. Watkins wrote a letter to the editor and asked him to stop printing that trash. The editor was from up east, though, and said the poems were very good but that only a small group could understand and appreciate them. Mr. Farney took this out of the paper and put it on the board in the room.

Mr. Farney liked plants. All over the windowsills in the room he had them in pots and jars. When one started to droop, he could just touch it with his thin fingers full of the light blue veins, and pull off the bad leaves so that the plant hardly shook at all, and the next few days he had it standing up straight again. He liked violets more than anything else because he told us they were shy and delicate. He could take violet plants and pick the violets right out from under the leaves where nobody else could ever find them.

Mr. Farney lived in a little house in town with another man who gave music lessons. It was painted blue and white and had pink curtains in the front windows. Both of them never were in the war. They were some of the few men who were left in town. The people who took music lessons from the other man said the house was pretty on the inside and had all light-colored things in it and plenty plants in pots. Mr. Farney's garden was the prettiest in town. Women used to ask him about how to grow this and that, and he always helped them because he was a very nice person. Mr. Farney called the other man "dear" once when they were in the drugstore together. Everybody heard about it sooner or later, and some laughed and some shook their heads and some wanted to see him leave the valley. But he was the best teacher our school ever had, so nothing ever came of it.

Maybe you would have thought Mr. Farney was alright if you didn't hear him talk. He sort of emphasized some words more than others, and he'd take a deep breath before he said anything. When he was talking, you always watched his hands because he used them a lot.

"*Now,*" he would say, "I hope you all can sit *still* for just a *little* minute while I get this record on. I *do* wish the state would send us a phonograph worth *mentioning.* The one I have at home is *so* much better. There. This is one of my *own* records, and it is a Beethoven quartet, Opus Eighteen, Number One. Notice the *homogeneity* of interpretation. Oh, I *do* wish that boy in the third row would stop *leering* at me. It's only *English* that I'm speaking. Tomorrow we *must* have a vocabulary review. *Do* remind me."

Nobody laughed at Mr. Farney when he spoke. He knew too much about things like classical music that we didn't know. I did think we had a little too much music that last year, though. That and poems. The poems he read to us were better than the music because most of them were pretty, but some of the music he played for us sounded off key, or like the instruments in the band were trying to outdo each other. Mr. Farney liked it, though, so it must have been good. One poem he read to us he made the whole class learn, and we recited it at graduation. It was by Henry Wadsworth Longfellow, and the only thing I knew he wrote was "Paul Revere's Ride," which we learned for Miss Moore because she said it was the only poem she ever heard that she liked. This one was different from "Paul Revere's Ride." It was the only beautiful thing I ever heard, especially one part:

> Then read from the treasured volume
> The poem of thy choice.
> And lend to the rhyme of the poet
> The beauty of thy voice.
> And the night shall be filled with music,
> And the cares, that infest the day,
> Shall fold their tents, like the Arabs,
> And as silently steal away.

I recited it for Aunt Mae, and she said it was beautiful, just like I thought. I didn't tell anybody in school that I liked it, or they would have thought I was crazy. Everybody learned it because they had to, but they thought it was stupid and wanted to sing a song instead. Mr. Farney said we could sing a song too, so that made them feel better. The class voted to sing "Dixie."

Our graduation night was really nice. Aunt Mae went with me and got that woman she knew from the time she worked at the plant named Flora to stay with Mother. Flora was happy because her son came back and married some girl from town instead of a Chinee like she thought he might. They lived with her down in town and had two children. One of them looked like Flora herself, the little boy.

We had the graduation in the hall on Main Street they always used for graduations and wedding receptions. All the lights were on, and they had flowers on the platform and twenty chairs out for our class to sit on. After Aunt Mae got her seat out front, I went up on the platform and sat where Mr. Farney had told me to. Some of the others in my class were already up there, and we said hello. We had been in the same class ever since Mrs. Watkins' room. I had on a suit we just bought and one of Poppa's old shirts. I was the first man in my family to get through eighth grade. Aunt Mae was sitting in about the fourth row. She had on a big hat that tilted to one side and a dress with yellow flowers all over it. A few little yellow curls came down on her forehead to right above her eyebrow. I thought of how good she looked for her age. The only thing wrong was her eyes. They looked tired and sad.

I saw all the people I knew sitting out there. Mr. and Mrs. Watkins were sitting next to the preacher, who was going to give a prayer tonight, but she looked up at the ceiling when she saw me looking at her. Miss Moore was in the front row where she could hear what was going to happen. Her old mother was with her, and she was deaf too, but she had a hearing aid she got in the capital sticking out of her ear, with the cord from it hanging down the front of her dress. One of

the women who testified at Bobbie Lee Taylor's the night I
went was sitting in the back talking to a little boy who must
have been hers. Bruce, the little boy Poppa sent me over to
visit, was graduating with me. I saw his mother out front,
and she saw me, and we just stared at each other. When
Poppa lost his job, Bruce's father stopped being friends with
him. I looked back at Aunt Mae and saw that the old man
who had the band was sitting next to her and they were
talking. I wondered what he was doing at my graduation.
Aunt Mae smiled at him a little bit, and I knew he must have
been telling jokes. He always told jokes. I never liked people
who always were telling jokes, especially ones like he told
that weren't even funny, and ones where they tried to imitate
people like he tried to imitate Negroes that didn't even
sound like Negroes. I know Aunt Mae didn't like him either.
She told me so. She'd look at him and listen and smile and
then turn her head away and make a face in the other
direction.

Pretty soon everybody was there, so we started. Mr. Farney
sat at the piano. The preacher got up and started to pray. His
back was to me, and I noticed how it was getting round. I
thought of how old he must have been getting. He was
almost fifty years old when we dropped off the rolls, and
that was when we moved onto the hill. He divorced his first
wife right before the war ended because he said she drank.
He married again a little while later. His second wife was an
organ player at some church in Memphis where a friend of
his was minister. She was in her twenties and pretty but a
little fat. They got married right on the preacher's radio
program by his friend. After it was over the friend started
joking about what a good organ player he lost, and I turned

off the radio. I don't know what happened to his first wife, but Aunt Mae told me she and her daughter were living in New Orleans, where the daughter was going to a Catholic school.

When the preacher finished we all sat down, and Mr. Farney talked about what a fine class we were and said he was glad to have had us for pupils. All the parents clapped. Then we sang "Dixie," and everybody sang with us, and Mr. Farney was wrinkling his nose at the piano. Then Mr. Farney gave us a certificate saying we had satisfactorily completed grade school and could enter any state high school with it, and he hoped we would do just that. We pledged allegiance to the flag and recited the poem. Everybody recited it too fast and ruined the whole thing. Then I was out of grade school.

I passed Miss Moore, and she said she was proud of me, and I went over to where Aunt Mae was waiting. She kissed me, and I looked around to see if anybody saw her, and I could feel myself turning red. Aunt Mae didn't see me do this, though. She was looking for something in her purse. When she brought it out, it was something wrapped like a present. I opened it up, and it was a watch, a real new one that must have cost at least thirty dollars. I thanked her and wondered where she could have got the money to buy it.

We went outside in the still night. It wasn't too hot, because the real hot weather didn't come to the valley until August, but it was just still with the sound of some kind of bug I didn't know the name of. People were coming out of the hall and nodding at Aunt Mae. Everybody knew her from her singing. I started to walk toward the hill, but Aunt Mae said, "Over here, David. Clyde's going to drive us to the hill." I hadn't noticed that he'd been with us all the time. There he was standing next to Aunt Mae. I wanted to walk, but I went with them to his truck.

"Here, David, get in." Aunt Mae held the door open for me, and I got up on the running board.

"No, Mae, there ain't enough room for him up here. Get in the back, boy, but watch out for my fiddle." Then I heard him say to Aunt Mae, "I bet he'd rather ride in the back than up here with us."

"You can ride up here if you want, David." Aunt Mae leaned out of the door. I knew Clyde didn't want it, so I said no and climbed up in the back. We started off, and I sat with my legs hanging down the tailgate. Main Street passed behind me. I looked down at the street and saw it flowing like the river flowed under the bridge at the old war plant when it was flooding. Cars going the other way passed by, and I watched them until their taillights turned into small red points down by the base of the other hill. The truck had a canvas roof and sides, so I couldn't see the stars or the houses passing alongside. Clyde's fiddle was hitting up against my back. I got mad that I didn't get up front like Aunt Mae said. I wanted to ride in a truck, but not in my suit with that big fiddle. I looked through the little window in the back of the cab where Clyde and Aunt Mae were. Clyde kept leaning over and trying to get his face under Aunt Mae's hat. Aunt Mae was almost out her door. I wondered if Clyde was watching the road. I never thought old men still liked women. The boys at school said they couldn't do anything anyway, so I wondered about Clyde again. He must have been a few years older than Aunt Mae, and she was getting old. The truck started going slower and slower.

Clyde kept his head under Aunt Mae's hat for almost a block. I heard Aunt Mae say something loud, and he came from under her hat and looked back at the road. Then a car went by the truck so close the canvas shook. I heard Aunt Mae really curse up front.

The truck stopped. We were at the bottom of the hill. I jumped down and just grabbed Clyde's fiddle before it fell out too. When I had it back in, I walked around to the door. Aunt Mae was saying, "Alright, Clyde, a little while." I put my hand on the door handle to let her out, but she said to me, "Look, honey, go wait there by the path for me. I'm going to stay here with Clyde for a while. Now, don't go off, you hear. I don't want to walk up the path alone. I won't be too long." She was going to say something else, but Clyde pulled her away from the window, so I went over to the path and waited.

The honeysuckle was thick around the old stumps there. It smelled wonderful and strong on the heavy, still air. There wasn't any breeze to blow it away the way it did sometimes. It just hung around there and got in your nose. I sat on one of the stumps and picked a few of the little flowers and smelled them, but you couldn't tell the difference from the air all around. The moon was shining on the honeysuckle and me and Clyde's truck. I looked over there once, but Clyde and Aunt Mae weren't sitting up. I couldn't see either one of them in the cab. I just saw the tip of Aunt Mae's hat sticking up by the window. I wondered what they were doing, and then I thought of when Aunt Mae went with George when I was little. I wondered if they did what the boys said at school. Aunt Mae was so old, though. She was sixty before we ever moved into the hills, and that was eight years ago when I went into Mrs. Watkins' for the first time.

I sat on the stump and looked up at the moon and down at Clyde's truck and smelled the honeysuckle, and I felt like I never felt before in my life. The warm air was all around me, sweet and still. It was so quiet and dark over by Clyde's truck. Clyde was doing something I never had done or even thought about much. Some of the boys at school went out with girls to the movies, but I never had. I never thought about taking one out. I didn't know any, living in the hills away from most of the town. I wondered if they'd like me if I asked them to go out. I was fourteen, and I never thought what I looked like. I knew I was getting tall, though.

Then I looked down at the watch Aunt Mae gave me, and I looked over at the truck. I heard her talking now, but I couldn't understand what she was saying. I didn't hear Clyde, but I could hear somebody breathing. Then Aunt Mae was quiet again. The watch said exactly eleven-thirty. I set it by the clock on the drugstore next to the hall where we had the graduation, and it was still running. It was hurting my wrist, so I loosened the leather band and wondered if it was real leather. Since the war everything was synthetic. They said after the war we were going to have plastic houses and helicopters, but I never saw any, and I wondered if they had them in New York. That was where they had everything.

I looked at the watch. It was ten of twelve. Clyde's truck was still quiet. I was getting mad at him. We should have been at the house about an hour ago to see how Flora was doing with Mother. Then Aunt Mae's hat came up all the way. I heard her cough. Clyde came up by the wheel. Aunt Mae said, "Good night, Clyde." She opened the door. Clyde didn't say anything but just started the motor. Aunt Mae got off the running board and closed the door. I heard Clyde trying to shift gears, but his truck was old, bought before the war, and he wasn't having too much luck. Aunt Mae walked over to where I was standing. She took my wrist and looked at the time and said, "Gee." We stood there and watched Clyde trying to get into first. The motor and the noise of the gears broke the still and the honeysuckle so much I wanted to go over and tell him to be quiet. I looked at Aunt Mae, and she was looking at the truck with that line around her mouth she always got when she was mad. Clyde got going at last. We watched him go off with his fiddle bouncing in the back.

We walked up the path. Aunt Mae said the honeysuckle smelled better than Clyde's breath. I didn't answer her because I didn't know what to say to something like that. We walked on a while longer, and I looked down at some of the houses where I knew they were having graduation parties. I wasn't invited to any. I stopped Aunt Mae and turned so the moonlight fell on my face, and I asked her how I looked. She looked at my face for a while, and then she put her hand at the back of my neck and said I was going to be fine-looking in about a year or so. My body was getting some lines, she said, and my face was getting to look like a man's too. We started walking again. I looked down at my suit. The moon was shining on the buttons of my coat. For the first time I noticed they weren't in a line with the opening of my coat. The suit was double-breasted. Then I remembered nobody at the graduation had a double-breasted suit. I was the only one. Most of the boys had on a sport coat with a different pair of pants, a different color, but they cost money.

It seemed like we just started, but before I knew it I heard the cinders under my feet, and I realized we were in the front yard. Aunt Mae stopped at the gate to rest. I waited with her for a while, then I walked on up the porch to see how Mother was. It was late, and maybe Flora had put her in bed. When I got to the door, it was wide open. I wondered what Flora had done that for. I could hear Mother talking in the kitchen, but I didn't hear anybody else. I stood on the porch and waited for Aunt Mae, and when I saw she was going to rest by the gate for quite a while, I called to her to hurry up and come in. She came across the cinders slowly, fanning herself with her big hat. When she got up to where I was on the porch and saw the door open, she looked at me and I told her how I had found it. She said Flora must have been crazy to let the door open like that with all the things in the hills that might run in. Mother was talking louder in the kitchen. We both heard her.

Aunt Mae went in and threw her hat on a chair in the front room while I closed the door. She turned around and said to me that Flora should have got Mother in bed long ago. The only voice I heard in the kitchen was still Mother's. She was answering somebody, it sounded like, only I didn't hear the other person. Aunt Mae was already in the kitchen when I got there, and I heard her asking Mother where Flora was. Mother was sitting at the table looking at the picture of the white crosses. Aunt Mae asked her again. She looked up like she was surprised to see Aunt Mae.

"Flora? Oh, yes. She told me I was crazy, Mae. Right to my face. Can you imagine that? Right to my face. She wasn't here thirty minutes. I've been sitting here waiting for you two to come in. Yes, Flora wasn't here thirty minutes."

Aunt Mae looked at Mother for a while, and I saw just how tired her eyes really were. Then she looked at me. And we just stood there under the one electric bulb and looked at each other and didn't say anything.

# Seven

I knew I wasn't going to high school, so I got a job down in town. It was at the drugstore, and it paid almost twenty dollars a week. I delivered and worked behind the counter selling things. I was lucky I got it, because it was a pretty good job. Aunt Mae was glad for me. She stayed with Mother in the daytime, but that wasn't much trouble. At night Clyde got her to go with the band. Most of the people in the valley had heard them, though, and they didn't get so much business anymore. When they did get jobs, it was usually someplace further away than the capital where people didn't know them. Then Aunt Mae would come in at almost four o'clock in the morning, and I'd wonder if it really took that long to drive back or if Clyde stopped along the way. Aunt Mae was really looking tired, I thought. If we didn't need the money, I never would have let her go out with him on the jobs. As it was, we didn't get much money from it anyway.

Flora went all over town and told everybody about Mother. Aunt Mae said she made a mistake in the first place asking her to come up to the house that night to take care of her. I knew if Flora didn't like Chinee people she wasn't going to like the way Mother was. Nobody in town would have known about it if it wasn't for Flora. Mother never went into town anyway, and nobody ever came up to our house, except Clyde sometimes, and he was always paying attention to Aunt Mae and ignoring everybody else. Plenty people in town got to wondering what went on up on the hill with Mother. Nobody in the valley acted strange aside from Mr. Farney, and that was different. People began to come right around the house to hunt until we put up a No Trespassing sign. That made them more curious, but it kept them away.

When I came in from the drugstore in the evening, I'd go into the cleared land behind the house to see Mother. The seedling pines were big now, and you never would think the land was ever cleared. Sometimes rabbits ran under them, and squirrels went up and down their trunks. Mother would be sitting down on the ground under the pines looking up at their branches. I'd sit and talk to her for a while, but I couldn't get her to say much anymore. She just looked at me with a faraway look and smiled. She smiled at everything I said, so after a while I stopped talking, and we would just sit in the pines and watch the sun go down and everything go dark. Then Aunt Mae would come out and sit a while. After that we went in for dinner. Aunt Mae would go upstairs and get ready the nights she had a job, and I'd sit with Mother in the kitchen and listen to the radio. Mother listened to the radio better than she listened to Aunt Mae or me. She followed all the stories and would say things while they were on, like "Just listen to the way that man goes on" or "Who do you think is the murderer, David?" Whoever I said, she would say, "No, I think you have the wrong one." And when the one I picked was the right one, she would say, "Oh, they were wrong about him."

One evening when I went back into the clearing, she got up off the ground and held me by the arm and pointed to the pines that were growing there and said, "You see how they're growing? They're your poppa's." Then she took me down to the front yard, and we stood on the cinders, and she pointed out over all the hills. "You see how they're growing?" I looked at the thousands of pines all over the valley. "From a little seed your poppa planted they're growing all over, but I saw them come up in his clearing first. I saw them first."

I liked the drugstore job. Mr. Williams, the man who owned it, gave me the job mainly because he had heard of Mother. Anyway, that's what I thought. He was nice that way, always trying to help people who needed it. He used to charge the people who lived on the street north of town a lot, but he let some of the poor people owe him for almost a year. I know because I delivered everything he sold. The ones on the street north of town never said anything about the high prices, and the poor ones were happy to get credit, so I guess it was alright.

You don't know how many people you can meet delivering for a drugstore—or, I guess, delivering for anything. They had all kinds. The women who lost their husbands in the war ordered things like Kleenex and hand lotion and Camay soap. I don't know why, but I almost always delivered things like that to them. They were still quiet, but none of them cried anymore. They always said, "Thank you, son," and didn't even seem to know I was there.

I delivered to Mr. Farney's house too. He ordered the expensive men's powders and aftershave things that nobody in town used. Mr. Williams got it from the company just for Mr. Farney and the other man he lived with who taught music. They came in the drugstore a lot because they liked to look around at everything, even the women's things. When one of them saw something he'd say, "Oh, come here and see this. Isn't this just precious." Mr. Farney always asked about Mother and said it was "tragic," which made me feel bad. But I knew Mr. Farney didn't know it made me feel that way. He wouldn't have said it if he knew I felt that way. Mr. Farney seemed to know when he said something to make you angry or make you feel bad. Then he'd say, "Oh, look at me. *Look* what I've done. Will you *ever* forgive me?" Then he would bite his nails or pick at his face.

One woman I delivered to was named Miss A. Scover. Anyway, that's the name she had on her doorbell. I had seen her before because she worked at the post office selling stamps. Her house was one of the new ones they were building up in the hills. She lived all alone for all I knew, except for a lot of cats that sat on the porch and went in the front door when she opened it. Sometimes she came to the door holding one in her arms. She would kiss it behind the ears and blow in its fur and say, "We're going outside, baby. Outside, outside."

She wasn't over forty years old. She didn't have any gray hair, but her face was thin, with a wrinkled sort of neck and a long nose. When I went there, she always came to the door in her robe. I wondered about it. No other woman in town would come out in her robe. After I gave her what she ordered, she said, "Come in, boy, while I get the money." I went in the first time, and it took about five minutes for her to find her purse. I called to the room where she was that I had to get back to the store. After a while she came out with the money and stared at me. I put out my hand, but she didn't give it to me. She asked how old I was, and I said I was fifteen. Then she asked if we delivered at night. I told her we did on Tuesdays and Thursdays. She didn't say anything, she just gave me the money, and I left. That night I told Aunt Mae about it. She looked at me with her eyes wide and said for me never to go in that house again.

The next week Miss Scover called Tuesday night and ordered some things. I was at the phone in the store. When I heard her voice, I hung up. She called a little while later, and Mr. Williams answered. I heard him say he couldn't understand it, sorry, must have been the operator's fault. He gave me the order, and I left before he gave me the address. When I got to the door, he called to me and asked if I knew where to go. I stopped and thought and said that I didn't. He called out the address I knew backwards, and the name too.

When I got up to Miss Scover's, all the cats were sitting out on the porch in the moonlight. They ran when I went up on the porch and rang the bell. Pretty soon Miss Scover came to the door. She had on a robe like she always wore, except this one looked more like silk or some expensive material. The light was shining out on the porch from the front room. Her face was in the shadow, and I couldn't see it, but she asked me to come in while she got her purse. I told her I had some valuable medicine in my bike basket and couldn't take my eyes off it for a minute. She said nobody around there was going to steal it, and anyway, it was damp outside. I told her no again, so she left to get the money. When she came back, she gave it to me and slammed the door. I got on my bike and rode down to the store and didn't think about Miss Scover again because she always came in the store after that to buy what she wanted.

When I wasn't delivering, I worked behind the counter with Mr. Williams. Sometimes he went out of the store and left me to take care of everything. That was the time I liked. I could look at everything we sold and act like I owned it. The boys I went to school with were mostly going to the high school. When they came in and saw Mr. Williams was gone, they asked me to show them some of the things they always made jokes about, but I didn't know where they were or where Mr. Williams kept them. Then they looked at me like I was silly and asked why I didn't find out and left the store. I wished I did know where they were. I didn't only want to be able to show them to the boys, I wanted to see what they looked like myself, I had heard so much at school about them.

The rest of the time mostly old women came into the store. They didn't always buy anything. They just looked around at the medicine we had on the shelves and read what they had in them and what they were for and how much you should take. Sometimes one would buy a bottle, then almost always return it the next day and say it didn't do her any good. I couldn't give the money back if it was already opened, and they had to open it to try it. Then they got mad and didn't come in again for about a week.

We sold magazines too. I think we were the only ones in town who did, except for the hotel. They sold mostly things like *Time* there, though. We sold movie magazines and comic books and magazines for women and some magazine some preacher in North Carolina put out. That sold pretty well, especially with the preacher's people. We sold more movie magazines than anything, though, those and the romance ones. We had a lot of comic books, but most people just looked at them and didn't buy. Even the old people looked at the comic books, especially the old men. They came in on Saturday afternoons and sat down on their haunches or sat on the floor and read them. By the time everybody had read all our comic books nobody wanted to buy them, so we lost money there. Mr. Williams didn't mind, though. They bought tobacco while they read, and we made a profit on it since they didn't grow it far away and Mr. Williams got it cheap.

The only thing I didn't like about the drugstore job was the people who asked about Mother, and plenty of them did. Even some who didn't know us but who heard about me from their friends asked. Some looked like they felt sorry. Most of them acted like they were afraid of Mother ever coming down into town and just asked me to be sure she was alright up on the hill. I didn't know what to say to the ones who felt sorry, but I told the others she never went far away from home and that they didn't have to worry. Then they said they weren't worrying, they just wanted to be sure she was happy and alright up there. I didn't like to hear people talk about Mother like this, just like she had a cold or fever and they hoped she wasn't suffering too much. I wondered if they thought how it made me feel. When one woman's daughter in town had a miscarriage, nobody even said a word about it. Nobody would ask the woman how her daughter was. That's how I felt about Mother, and I hoped they'd stop talking about it and asking me. I told some of Mother's old friends she knew when we lived down in town that maybe Mother would like to see them if they'd go and visit her, but they all gave some excuse about not feeling good enough to climb the hill, or else they had to take care of their house or something. Most of them never asked about Mother after that.

Flora came in the store a lot to buy baby things for her grandchildren, but she always got Mr. Williams to wait on her. When he wasn't in, she came back when he was. She never talked to me, and turned her face away when I looked at her. Aunt Mae told me she slapped Flora in the face the next time she saw her after the night I graduated. Then Flora began to cry and said she got frightened when she heard Mother talking the way she did, and ran out the house when Mother showed her the picture of the white crosses. Flora showed Aunt Mae a place on her leg where she slipped running down the hill. I looked at it every time Flora came in the store. It was a scar now, and it went almost all the way on her left leg from her knee to her ankle. Aunt Mae told me she felt sorry for Flora then and let her go from the way she had been holding her.

Flora must have spent all her money on the grand-children. She bought them toys and the little books we sold and all the new baby medicines. I thought it was probably because she was so happy they weren't Chinee. I thought she would have been luckier, too, to get a Chinee daughter-in-law than the ugly one she had. Nobody liked Flora's daughter-in-law except Flora and her son. She didn't even get out of eighth grade, and she was only fifteen when she married Flora's son. Mr. Farney told our class once that that girl was the worst pupil he ever had. I never spoke to her, but I always saw her on the street with those red pimples she had all over her face, even some on her arms.

It was about that time Jo Lynne began coming into the store. She was the granddaughter of some old man I used to see walking around town. Mr. Williams told me she was visiting the old man with her mother and that they were from someplace about fifty miles away, near the state line. When I first saw her, I knew she wasn't from the valley, because she was about my age but I never saw her around school or around the street.

The first day she came into the store I thought I knew her from somewhere at first. Her face looked like someone's face I had seen before. She looked at me, and I looked away, but I don't know why. I wanted to look at her again and see her eyes. They were sort of greenish-blue with dashes of gray that seemed to come out of their center. And it looked like you could see through them to the back of her eye.

Mr. Williams was in the back, so I had to wait on her. I went over to the medicine counter where she was standing, and she gave me a prescription she said she wanted for her grandfather. After I went back to give it to Mr. Williams, I was afraid to go back into the store where she was. I don't know why. I wanted to, because I wanted to have her look at me with her eyes again, but I just stayed around the prescription room. Mr. Williams saw me walking around behind him looking at the labels he had on all the bottles there, and he told me to get back into the store and tell that girl he'd have the prescription ready in a little while.

When I came down in the store again, she was reading one of the comic books from the magazine shelf. I told her the prescription would be ready in a little while, and she said okay, she'd wait. I wanted to go back up in the room with Mr. Williams, because every now and then she looked over at me where I was sitting on a stool behind the counter, and I scraped my feet along the floor and started to whistle and looked the other way.

When she went back to her comic book, I looked at her. She was about sixteen, maybe a little older, but I couldn't say how much. Only a few people in the valley had black hair. I didn't see it very often, so I looked at hers. Hers was prettier than most people's. It was long and wavy and shiny. She had some curls on her forehead, and then it was straight until her shoulders, where she had some more curls. Her eyebrows and eyelashes were black too, but her skin was white. Not only her face, but her arms too. Plenty women in the valley got their faces white, but their arms were still red.

She was pretty and could have been on the front of a magazine if it wasn't for her mouth. It was just a little too big, but I liked the way her lips curved. She had on a pretty color lipstick that looked red when the light was on her lips but looked purple when she was in the dark. I liked it with her eyes and hair.

Her breasts were big for only about sixteen, and high too. She was wearing a dress with a flower pattern on it that I didn't like, but it didn't look bad on her. I liked the way her big belt made her waist look real small. It looked like you could put your hands around it and your fingers would touch. I looked through her sandals and saw even the skin on her feet was white and soft. She looked at me just then. I looked away and began scraping my foot again.

Mr. Williams came down into the store a little while later with the prescription. He gave it to her and told her something about when to take it while I rang it up on the cash register. I stood next to Mr. Williams and listened to what he was telling her, and I noticed something I never noticed before: I was taller than Mr. Williams. I looked down at the girl. She was looking at Mr. Williams, but all of a sudden she looked up at me, and I saw her eyes again.

I saw her in the store a lot after that first day. She read the magazines and comic books while Mr. Williams filled the prescriptions for her grandfather. Sometimes she wore shorts, and I saw her legs were even whiter than the rest of her body, especially up near her thigh. And her knees weren't rough like the other girls in the valley, who had hard gray-looking knees. They were soft and white and had just one little crease in them.

After she had been coming in for about a month, I spoke to her one day. She started talking, though. I was just sitting behind the counter looking at her.

"Do you have this month's *Modern Romance*?" She was looking through the magazines.

I came from behind the counter and went over to the shelf. I began to tell her that I'd look for it, but my voice sounded strange to me, so I stopped and cleared my throat. She looked at me.

"I asked if you had this month's *Modern Romance*."

"Yes, I know. I don't know if we have it, but I'll look."

I started going through the magazines, and she said, "Thanks." Whenever someone is looking at me from behind, I seem to know it, and I knew she was looking at me now.

"Do you work here all the time?"

She had her hand resting on the shelf near my head, and I looked at its whiteness.

"Yes, I do. All the time the store's open and from thirty minutes before it does."

"How old are you, about nineteen?"

I stopped going through the pile of magazines. I turned around and looked at her. I started to tell her I was only about her age, but I thought of how tall I was, and I couldn't keep from looking in her eyes.

"Yes, just about. Nineteen and a half."

We looked at each other for a while and didn't say anything. Then she looked back at the pile of magazines. I turned around and started going through them again. After that she kept quiet, so I started talking.

"You're from out of the valley, aren't you?"

"Yes, my mother came here to take care of her father, Grandpa. He's been getting along poorly. If he gets better, we're going home again—Springhill."

"That's where you're from?"

"Yes. You ever been there?"

"No, I've never been out of the valley."

"Well, if you ever do get out, don't go there. This place is prettier."

I was surprised to hear anyone say the valley was pretty. I never thought much about it, but I was happy to be talking with her, so I went along with what she said.

Mr. Williams was done with the prescription before I

could find her magazine, so she paid and left. Mr. Williams went back into the other room. A few seconds later, the front door opened again, and she stuck her head in.

"I forgot to tell you goodbye."

"Oh, goodbye."

"Goodbye. I'll be in again if Grandpa has another prescription."

She smiled and closed the door. I smiled too, and was still smiling when Mr. Williams came in again. He asked me what I was smiling for, and I told him nothing.

I thought about her all the time after that. When Mother and I listened to the radio at night, I didn't hear what they were saying, and when she asked me something about the program, I usually couldn't answer her. She finally told Aunt Mae I didn't care about her anymore and cried and laid her head on the kitchen table. I didn't know what to tell Aunt Mae, but she didn't fuss about it because she knew the way Mother was.

A few nights after that, Aunt Mae and I were sitting on the porch. Mother was asleep upstairs. It was one of the nights Aunt Mae wasn't with Clyde. I hadn't been with her alone for a long while, and I wanted to talk. We sat and talked about everything, almost. The town was growing, and that was what we were talking about just then.

All up the hills where there were pines just a year ago houses were being built. Some big ones, but mostly little small ones that looked like boxes. The veterans all had children now, and they couldn't live with their families down in town anymore, so they were moving into the hills. Some were starting at the foot of our hill. When I went down the path to the store, I could see the little foundations being laid a short distance from the street they were cutting there. Our hill wasn't being improved as fast as some, though. It was too steep to build on very well, and it was too full of clay, they said. That made me happy. We had been on the hill for so long I didn't want to see it full of those little homes. I wondered what was going to happen to them down there at the foot of the hill when a good rain came. That's where the clay was really soft, where the water stayed after it had come all the way down from about where we lived.

Aunt Mae was looking at the other hills. The one across town from where we lived was almost full of those little houses now, all the same white kind. The hill to the side of ours was really developed too. Even in the dark we could see the path of the roads they were cutting on it that made it look like the crossword puzzles Mr. Farney used to try to get us to work, but no one knew enough words to fill them out.

All of a sudden I told Aunt Mae I saw a girl in the store that I really liked.

"I was wondering when you were going to say something like that, hon."

Aunt Mae stopped rocking, and I wondered if she was mad.

"Why don't you ask her out, Dave? All the other boys and girls I see down in town have been going out for a long time. You can't sit up here every night with your Mother like you do."

"I don't mind it, and besides . . ."

"Yes, I know, hon. But look at how old you are now. It isn't natural for you to be here every night with her. I shouldn't have let it go on like it has, but Clyde's been getting us some good jobs, you know. We couldn't let her in the house alone."

"I know that, Aunt Mae, that's . . ."

"No, no. Listen to me. You know I'm home some nights. You ask this girl out, and I'll make it my business to be here that night and look after Mother."

I didn't say anything just then. She started rocking again.

"Suppose she won't go out with me."

"Don't worry, Dave, she will. You're a nice-looking boy. You're tall, that's for sure. You look better than those little kids I see coming into the roadhouse when I sing there."

"I don't have any money like they do, Aunt Mae. It costs a lot to go to the roadhouse. You have to buy beer, and you have to use a car to get there."

"Well, go to a show in town, then. How much is it? Thirty cents apiece? Well, that's sixty cents there, and that isn't much. Even I got that much."

She started laughing, but I didn't feel like laughing with her. I wondered if Jo Lynne would want to go just to the movie.

"Do you think she'll go if I ask her, Aunt Mae?"

"I think she will. Anyway, there's no harm in asking."

It sounded easy the way Aunt Mae spoke about it, but I didn't ask Jo Lynne for a while. I waited until she came in two times after that, and then I did. She said she could, and I was surprised.

The night we were going out Aunt Mae stayed home with Mother. I knew Clyde had a good job for them that night, but Aunt Mae said the place was almost seventy miles away and she didn't mind missing it. I wore a flowered shirt I bought in town and a pair of Poppa's good pants he bought before the war. When I left the house, Mother saw them on me and said she thought she saw them someplace before.

Aunt Mae told her they were new, though, so I told them both good night.

Jo Lynne was waiting for me down in town on Main. She said it would be better if we met somewhere instead of me going to her grandfather's house to get her. He didn't want her to go out, she said, and it would have made trouble. It didn't matter to me. I was glad I didn't have to go meet him and her mother.

She was on the corner where she said she would be. I thought she looked good. Her hair was tied back with a green ribbon, and she had on a flowery sort of dress and sandals. That lipstick she used made her lips look dark at night, dark purple. It was a hot night, and there were a lot of people on Main walking around. Some of the men who were crossing the corner where she was turned around after they passed her and looked at her. The women looked at her too, because she looked different from them, and they knew she was a stranger in town and probably wondered where she was from. The breeze that was coming up Main blew her skirt and the ribbon in her hair just a little. I liked the way it did that.

She smiled when she saw me. We stood there and spoke for a while, then we started for the movie, which was two blocks down. I said hello to some people I knew, most from the drugstore, but Jo Lynne didn't know anyone to say hello to. They all looked at us, though, because they thought I stayed up on the hill with Mother all the time.

I don't remember what the movie was. It was one of those cheap ones they always showed on Saturday nights with gangsters or cowboys. Some people who went to school with me and who went to the high school now were in the show with girls. I knew they always went on Saturdays, then went to the roadhouse after and danced and drank. When I saw them, I wished I had a car so we could go out there too. Everyone said it was a lot of fun.

It was hot in the show, and it smelled like always. The old fans they had to keep it cool made so much noise that you couldn't hear the actors sometimes. All the little children were sitting up in the first and second row about three feet from the screen. I never thought about them too much before, but they bothered me tonight, always running up and down the aisle and talking and throwing things up at the screen. I wished the sheriff's brother would come get them and put them out, but he charged more on Saturday nights, and if he put them out, he had to give their money back.

Jo Lynne's arm was touching mine. I couldn't keep my mind on the movie, but I kept looking at the screen. The actors moved around and talked and shot at each other, but I didn't know what the story was about. I looked down at her once. The white light from the screen was shining on her lips, and they were wet, and I wondered why. She didn't notice me looking. She kept looking at the movie. I looked from her face down to where her arm was touching mine. It was white, and it felt soft and smooth. After a while I took her hand, which was hanging over the arm of her chair, and held it. She didn't even look at me, but she tightened her fingers over my hand, and I was surprised.

The movie ended, and everybody started getting up. Only the little children in the first and second row stayed in their seats, but they always stayed for two movies. They were hitting on each other and screaming, and I wondered where their mothers were. Jo Lynne and I got up. My hand was wet from having held hers. I wiped it on Poppa's old pants, and it stained them, so I held my hand over the spot till we got out.

When we were out on the street, Jo Lynne said she thought the movie was good. I said I liked it too and asked her where she wanted to go. I wanted to take her to the restaurant, but she said her grandfather didn't want her coming home too late. She said she'd rather go for a walk.

The breeze was still blowing, and it was a little cooler. We started off down to where she lived. I held her hand, and she didn't say anything. She squeezed it again like she did in the show. We talked a little about the movie. I didn't remember much about it, so I went along with what she said and agreed with her. After we finished talking about that, she said she was glad I asked her to go out because she got tired of sitting at her grandfather's every night. I didn't tell her I was surprised she said she would go, and I let it go at that.

I didn't know why I felt frightened. I just did. We were walking along not saying anything for a long while, and I couldn't think of anything to say to start a conversation. I felt silly holding her hand and not saying anything, but Jo Lynne didn't try to speak either. Maybe she didn't have anything to say too. I don't know. I just know we were getting closer to her grandfather's house. It was near the base of the hill across from ours.

When we turned into the street where it was, Jo Lynne looked up at the hill. They were building some of those new houses up on it. You could count how many they had up there by the roofs, because they were shining under the moon. I could see about fifteen built, but I knew they had some sides up without roofs yet. Before we got to her grand-father's, Jo Lynne stopped and held on to my hand hard. I looked down at her. She was looking up on the hill at the shining roofs.

"Let's go up and see those houses they're building, David."

I looked down at her again, only this time she was looking up at me.

"I thought your grandfather wanted you home."

She held on to my hand harder until I thought the blood in it would stop. I looked at her purple lips. They were still wet, and I wondered about them again.

"We won't be up there long. I just want to see what's been going on."

I said okay, so we went up the path the workmen and the trucks used. It had a lot of ruts, and Jo Lynne almost tripped sometimes, but I grabbed her by the waist and kept her from falling. It surprised me to find how soft her waist was. Aunt Mae's was hard and the same shape all the time.

We got up to the first little group of houses and looked around. Jo Lynne kept close to me because she said she was afraid to be in the hills at night and if it wasn't for me she wouldn't have come. It made me feel good to hear her say that.

It looked funny to see the little houses all empty with the doors and windows open. In a few days, they would all be closed with wood and glass, and it would be a crime to go into them then. I thought of what a difference there was between these little wooden boxes now with the moonlight shining through where the doors should be and what they'd be in a little while with people living in them and loving them for a home.

We sat down on the steps of one of the little houses. Everything smelled like fresh-cut pine and green wood and plaster, that funny dry smell of plaster that you thought would choke you. They had cleared almost all the pines down here, and the browning stumps stuck up all around us and combed out the breeze that blew through our hair.

Jo Lynne was quiet. The breeze blew through her hair, and I could hear her breathing the strong pine air. I put my arm around her. She looked up at me, and I saw her wet purple lips even in the dark. I saw the moonlight on their wet, with little cracks of dark between. She looked at me in a different way, like I had never seen her look, and I knew what to do. I kissed her.

# Eight

Then Jo Lynne left. Her grandfather got better, and her mother said they could go back to Springhill. I remember the day she came in the store and told me. It was one of those times Mr. Williams was out, and I was moving some shampoo bottles around under the counter trying to clean up. I had heard the door close and the footsteps come across the old tile floor. It was a sort of slopping walk, and only one person I knew walked like that. I got up and saw Jo Lynne looking around, looking for me.

When I saw her face, I knew something was wrong. She didn't wait, though, she came right out and told me that she and her mother were planning to leave. I didn't answer her. When things like that happen to me, I just don't speak. I don't know what to say. I just looked up at the shelf next to me and thought a while about nothing. For a while my eye read the label on one of the bottles there. Then I heard Jo Lynne talking again. I was surprised to hear her talk that way, like it was any ordinary thing you could just talk about like the weather or the new houses on the hills. That night up in the new houses came into my mind, when her lips were purple and the moonlight was shining on their wet and I could see the little cracks in them thinner than a pin.

When she finished talking, I gathered that she was leaving the next day on the train. I came out from behind the counter and grabbed at her hand, but it felt different from the other night when it made mine so hot it sweated. She didn't look at my face. Her eyes were turned to the side, and she watched the people on the street who were passing by the big plate glass window not even thinking about what was going on inside the drugstore. I hoped nobody came in, because I wanted to talk to her when I was ready and could think of what to say.

She pulled her hand away and said that, well, she'd said all there was to say. It sounded something like a movie to me, like what they said in those cheap Friday night movies with the actors you never heard of. I grabbed her hand again when I saw she was going to leave. I asked her if she was going to come to town again or if I could write letters to her at her house. She turned away from the window and looked at me and said she might be coming to town again sometime. I asked her when.

"I don't know. Maybe if my grandfather gets sick again," she said, and tried to pull her hand away again, but I held her.

"Well, where can I write you? I have some paper here. Let me write it down."

"No, Mother won't want to see me getting letters from some boy. What's the matter with you, anyway? We just went out once. Let go of my hand. You act like you don't know any girls at all. I see . . ."

"I don't know any girls, I really don't. You're the only one I know. I don't . . ."

"Oh, keep quiet. And let me go now. It sounds like you want to get married."

"We could get married, Jo Lynne. The state'll marry us. You're almost seventeen, and I'm old . . ."

Jo Lynne hit me in the face with her free hand. Her face was red, and her eyes were wild, and I saw I was getting her scared, so I let her go. She fell down on the tiles, and I went to pick her up, but she was at the door before I could even bend over to get her. She was crying and screaming I was crazy when she slammed the door. I watched her from the window as she ran down Main with her hair flying. Then a woman passed the window and looked in at me and stared. I wondered why she didn't go away. She pointed to her cheek, but I didn't understand her, so I walked away from the window and passed the mirror. When I saw my face, I knew why she had been pointing. My cheek was beginning to bleed in the hollow where I was hit.

I ran behind the counter to where Mr. Williams kept the bandages in a box and got out one and pressed it to my cheek over the thin little scratches her nails made. My face was burning. I felt my eyes pounding against the lids like they wanted to get out, and my hair felt like wool that I wanted to tear off to cool myself.

When I got my mind steady, I began to think about what had happened. Sitting on the high stool behind the counter,

I looked around the store and out onto the bright street. I wondered where Jo Lynne was, if she was home. Then I thought of myself and how dumb I was. I'd made a fool out of myself the night we went out, and it didn't even matter to her. The night up in the new houses didn't matter. Kissing her didn't matter either. She didn't know what I thought when I saw the moon on her face, or when my arm touched hers in the movie, or even when I heard her walk into the drugstore a little while before. She didn't know she was the only thing I ever wanted to have that I thought I'd get.

I took the bandage off and looked at the red lines on my cheek. They made a sort of tit-tat-toe pattern like we used to make on the blackboard at school when I was little. I felt ashamed when I looked at it. Someone hitting me. I never did anything to make anyone hit me, except for Bruce before I went to school. I wondered what people would think if they knew someone hit me, especially a girl. They'd think all kinds of dirty things like people always did. Or maybe they'd be surprised, too, because they thought I was just a quiet boy who worked at the drugstore and lived with my aunt and my mother up on the hill in an old house, and sat up there with my mother every night and took care of her and listened to the radio with her.

I went and looked in the mirror again. There were two dark red lines on my cheek right above where I shaved. The blood had stopped flowing now, so I knew that was what they were going to look like for the rest of today, anyway. Then I tried to think of some kind of excuse to give the people who might see me, but I couldn't think of anything that sounded like you could believe it. I didn't care, either.

Mr. Williams kept some matches behind the counter, so I

took one and lit the bandage and threw it in the trash basket. I watched the smoke curl up, gray and fast at first, then white and slow. When it stopped, I began to smell the burnt smell. I breathed it in and sat up on the stool and didn't think about anything. My mind was empty.

Work in the drugstore went on like always. Mr. Williams had the old front torn off and put all glass in the place where the old bricks were. That made business pick up some, just like he said it would. I don't guess he ever thought of what it would be like in the store when the sun was going down and it was shining right in through all that glass. That was the time the store got all orange inside, and it hurt your eyes to look at almost anything. Then he had to spend a lot more money buying shades, and that messed up the way it was supposed to look.

Around this time Aunt Mae began to change. She had always been nice to me, but she was even better now. I never told her about what happened with Jo Lynne, so she didn't have to feel sorry for me, but it seemed to me that she did, and I wondered why.

Thinking people feel sorry for you is something I guess you should appreciate, but I didn't and never have. It made me mad to see someone acting like I was pitiful, always asking how I was, fixing special things for me, talking to me in a sort of baby way, making her eyes all sorry-looking when she looked at me. I wanted to tell Aunt Mae she got me mad, and I wanted to ask her why she treated me in such a different way, but somehow or another, I never did. I just stayed curious and waited to see what was making her act like I was a crippled little mountain rabbit that hadn't had anything to eat for a week.

Sometimes when I went home at night I just went up to the old room where my train was. I could open the window up there and prop it up with a broom pole and look out at the stars and the pine tips. I could feel the breeze blowing into the room, stirring the dust off everything and pushing the old, stale air around. Aunt Mae wasn't around to pat me on the head and feed me the special things she made and look at me with that look that made me mad. I could think up there too.

I could think about plenty things. Everybody who left grade school with me was at the state university now, at least all who went to high school, and most did. People who came into the drugstore always talked about them, what a good time they were having, how some were in fraternities and sororities if they had money, how this one was studying to be a doctor or something else you had to go to college to be. I thought of what I was ever going to be. I couldn't stay at the drugstore all my life, and there wasn't much else I could do in the valley. You had to go to college to be anything. But I didn't even get near high school, and almost everybody got that far.

I thought about Jo Lynne too. I didn't like to think about it, but I did. The night I went out with her was the best time I had since I was in school or during the war at the propeller factory party. When I thought of the day in the drugstore, my face got hot and my eyes began to pound again. I could feel my heart beat all over my body. That was a day I wanted never to remember, but every time I got up in the room and let my mind go over things, it came back to me as clear as if I was right there getting hit.

Maybe I could have told Aunt Mae about Jo Lynne. It was the way she was acting to me that made me not tell her. If Aunt Mae had been like she was before, I would have told her, but I didn't want her to know about it, not anything about it. I was tired enough of what she was doing now, and I didn't want her to get worse when I told her how I missed Jo Lynne and wished I could write her and try to make some excuses and say I was sorry about what I had said and done and ask her to write me a letter back, even if she was still mad, just as long as I got something from her that I could see her writing on. I wanted to go by her grandfather's and get the place where she lived, but I never could do it. Maybe if I would have talked to Aunt Mae she would have told me the right thing to do, but I didn't want to talk to her about anything like that right now.

So I just sat up there in the old room and looked out at the pine tips sticking up near the stars, or at my old train that didn't run anymore but just stood there all tan from rust and rusted to the track from the leaky roof. I sat there and thought that someday I would get to work on it and get it loose and oil it, and maybe it would run again.

When I sat up there nights, I could hear the radio playing under me and Mother asking questions and Aunt Mae answering her. Aunt Mae was home nights now. Clyde went to Nashville to see some man who might give him a job on the radio there, on a music program. Every day I saw a letter around the house he wrote Aunt Mae. I could tell they were Clyde's letters because they were printed. Clyde didn't know how to write, at least I didn't think so, because I never saw him do anything but print. Aunt Mae never said when he was coming back, and I didn't care. I was glad to have her home nights to sit with Mother, even though we needed the money.

But Mother was changing, I thought. She didn't look like she did once. She got skinnier and skinnier, and her cheeks began to sink in. The skin was stretched over her nose until it looked like just an onion peel covered the bone. That's why I was glad Aunt Mae was home, so I could get upstairs. I didn't like to sit in the half-dark with her and listen to the radio. It got me scared to look at her and see her look at me with that black under her eyes. When I was around, she just looked at me, and that made me feel uncomfortable. Even when we were eating. She wouldn't eat if I was at the table with her. She just sat there with the food in front of her and stared at me. After she did this a while, Aunt Mae had to give us our food at a different time so both of us could eat, because I couldn't eat either with her staring at me.

I got mad at myself for feeling that way about my own mother, but then I thought about it, and I told myself she wasn't a real mother anymore. She was just a strange woman who frightened me and didn't seem to know me at all. She didn't even look like my mother. I knew what my mother looked like. I remembered the woman who put me to bed and danced with me at the factory party and stood with me when my poppa went off to war. I remembered the woman who looked at the train until long after it was gone with Poppa on it. But this wasn't the same one. This was a woman that I was scared to be in the same house with. She never talked to me now. She just sat and looked and made me scared.

And I knew what was happening down in town. It was a long time since I graduated from grade school and we got Flora to sit with Mother. After that everybody in town knew about her. They were pretty nice about it, and after they saw I wasn't going to talk about it too, they never said anything else to me. But I knew the way the people in town thought about things. They always had some time left over from their life to bother about other people and what they did. They thought they had to get together to help other people out, like the time they got together about the woman who let a colored man borrow her car and told her the best place for her was up north with all the other nigger lovers, and the time they got the veterans with overseas wives out. If you were different from anybody in town, you had to get out. That's why everybody was so much alike. The way they talked, what they did, what they liked, what they hated. If somebody got to hate something and he was the right person, everybody had to hate it too, or people began to hate the ones who didn't hate it. They used to tell us in school to think for yourself, but you couldn't do that in the town. You had to think what your father thought all his life, and that was what everybody thought.

I knew what everybody thought about Mother. She didn't have any more friends down in town to say any different, so Flora's story got bigger and bigger. I knew Flora was back with the preacher and was even the head of the big people's Sunday school. It was too bad if the preacher got to be the leader in anything. Except for Bobbie Lee Taylor, everything he planned always came off right the way he wanted. When he wanted to send people out of town, they went, especially if they didn't belong to the church.

The preacher was the head of the people that decided

who was going to the state institutions like the crazy house and the poor folks' asylum. Every year he sent about one old man or woman away to the old asylum, but they didn't want to go. Everybody said you died there pretty soon, and even if the people were real old, they didn't want to die, and they cried when the preacher took them down to the train. If they didn't mind too much, he drove them to the place in his car, but those were the ones who believed him and thought it was really as nice as he said, or else they were deaf and couldn't know what was going on anyway. I saw an old woman once who couldn't move herself at all, and she couldn't even speak. One day when I was going home from the drugstore I saw the preacher take her into his car from the old place where she lived. She couldn't move or speak or anything, but her eyes were the most awful thing I ever saw anytime in my life. When I passed the car, she looked at me with a real scared look like a little mountain rabbit has when it sees it can't get away from the thing that's hunting it. I don't know why I did, but I stood there after the preacher's car left and watched it go down the street with that old woman. I guess she's still there now in the state poor home.

Mr. Williams' wife went to the preacher's church, and that's how I found out about Mother. Mr. Williams told me the preacher and Flora were trying to see if they could get the crazy house to take Mother in. I didn't believe it when I heard it, because Mother never even saw any people in town, and nobody even saw her except for some men who still came up into the clearing to get rabbits. I tried to think of why they wanted to do a thing like that, but I couldn't think up a reason. Mr. Williams told me to tell Aunt Mae about it, because they couldn't do anything if the family wouldn't let them. I wanted to tell Aunt Mae, but lately I didn't speak with her much, so I never did. I thought about it a lot when I sat upstairs, though. I thought about how some people could do what they wanted to another person and not get put in jail by the sheriff, and I thought about Mother getting in the preacher's car and going off. That got my mind all filled up. I couldn't think about anything else when I thought about those two driving away and the preacher telling everybody after how he helped the town and helped a poor woman. But, he would say, it was only the Christian thing to do, and any good Christian would leap at doing such a thing.

I was getting tired about what the preacher called Christian. Anything he did was Christian, and the people in his church believed it, too. If he stole some book he didn't like from the library, or made the radio station play only part of the day on Sunday, or took somebody off to the state poor home, he called it Christian. I never had much religious training, and I never went to Sunday school because we didn't belong to the church when I was old enough to go, but I thought I knew what believing in Christ meant, and it wasn't half the things the preacher did. I called Aunt Mae a good Christian, but nobody else in the valley would have because she never went to church. One day I told somebody I thought Aunt Mae was just as much a Christian as Mrs. Watkins claimed to be. It was a woman who came into the store a lot. She got to talking about some people in town, and when she came to Mrs. Watkins she said that that was a real, dedicated Christian. When I said Aunt Mae was too, she said I was a babe who didn't know the true word, or something like that in the kind of words church people use.

When Mr. Williams didn't say any more about Flora and

the preacher and Mother, it passed from my mind in a little while. But things like Jo Lynne and the way Aunt Mae was acting didn't. I still thought about Jo Lynne when I sat upstairs. Not from the windows in the room where the train was, but from the windows in my bedroom, you could see the little houses on the hill where I kissed her. They were all finished now, and they had a lot of people in them. They were lighted at night now. That made them even easier to find, and at night I would sit on the windowsill sometimes and look off at them. But I didn't like to see that part of the hill lighted up. I liked to think about it like it was the night we were there, with the houses all empty and the hill with nobody but us on it and the moonlight the only thing besides the dark. I even wondered who was living in the house where we sat on the step.

Then I stopped worrying about Aunt Mae. One day when I came in from the store she was sitting in the kitchen running her hands along the oilcloth on the table.

"Come in here, hon," she said when she heard me coming in the house. I felt like going right up to the train room, because I didn't feel like being around her with the sorry eyes. When she heard me start up the stairs, she called again. "Come here, hon. In the kitchen."

I went in there, and she had a faraway look. She was looking out the back door into the clearing where I guess Mother was somewhere in the pines, which were large enough now to compare with any in the hills.

"Sit down. Here by the table. Mother's back there." She pushed a chair out for me with her foot. "Well, how was work today?"

"Okay, Aunt Mae."

"What's the matter?"

"Nothing. Things were just slow. Nobody came in hardly, excepting some old lady who always does and asks for things half-price."

She looked at me for a while, and that was why I didn't feel like going and talking with her. I looked the other way so I wouldn't see her eyes.

"I got something to tell you, Dave."

I saw her hand go across the table to some paper I never noticed before. It was a letter, or it must have been, because it was in an envelope.

"I got a letter from Clyde today that I'm going to read to you."

I didn't say anything, and she handed it to me.

"Here, you read it for yourself, hon."

I opened the envelope and took out the letter. It was printed in red pencil on old tan line paper like I used to use in grade school with Mrs. Watkins.

> Dear Mae,
>
> I have got good news for us. Bill here says he will use us on his radio show. If he likes us. I think he will Mae. You don't have to hurry here. You got a week to make it. I have a nice room here. Bill says maybe we can make records to. Theres a lot of money in them. I know. You will like Nashville. You said you have never been here. They got all kinds of radio shows. Write me a letter love and say when you will get here. This is a big chance.
>
> With Love,
> Clyde

After I finished it, I read it again. It still said the same thing, and it sounded crazy to me. I looked at Aunt Mae, but she wasn't sitting at the table. She was washing some dishes over at the sink. After a while she turned around.

"Well, hon, what do you think about it?"

"I don't know, Aunt Mae. What does it mean?"

"Clyde thinks he can get us a good job, a permanent one, in Nashville on the radio or records."

Nashville. That sounded strange to me. Aunt Mae in Nashville.

"What about me and Mother?"

"That's it, hon. That's what I'm afraid about, but if we get a job, I can send for you two. This man Bill told Clyde it wouldn't be long before he could get us something. Don't you see? I can make a lot of money."

The whole thing sounded funny to me. Aunt Mae in Nashville with Clyde. She didn't know how long she was going to be. And Mother. What would I do with her? I was scared of her even with Aunt Mae around. And what would we eat? I still didn't say anything to Aunt Mae, though.

"Look, hon, I'm taking the bus out of here the day after tomorrow. And don't worry. It won't be long before you and Mother get a train ticket from me, you hear?"

All at once the whole thing hit me the way it should have at first. She was really planning to leave me with Mother. My mind got all filled again, and I looked up at Aunt Mae.

"But what am I going to do with Mother? I work all day, and she's up here, and what are we going to eat? If I was . . ."

"There's nothing to worry about, hon, really. I been with her all day. She just sits in your poppa's old cabbage patch or somewhere around the house. She isn't trouble. I know you can leave her here all day and she won't get in trouble."

I tried to think about what Aunt Mae was saying, but I couldn't. I just knew she really meant she was going. If I knew about it a week before or something, maybe I could think about what to do around the house while she was gone, but this was all of a sudden. I was really going to be left in the house with Mother to do everything for her. Aunt Mae in Nashville and Poppa in Italy and me here with Mother. It all ran together in my mind so fast I couldn't stop any of it long enough to think on it. I just looked down at the oilcloth. It was the same oilcloth on the table for as long as we lived in the house, but the shiny top part was wearing away in little creases and lines all over it, and the stiff cloth underneath was showing. I ran my fingers over the little cloth parts and let the rough rub on my skin. It felt so different from the slippery oilcloth.

"Look, hon. Maybe I shouldn't do this, but I never had a chance like it before, even when I was young. I can get on the radio and records. Are you listening, Dave? It don't seem like you hear anything I'm saying. Look. Quit your job at the store. Then you can stay here all day with Mother, you hear? In a week, or maybe two, you'll get the tickets to Nashville from me. And Dave, when you get to Nashville, maybe you can go back to school at one of the good ones they have there. Cities have good schools, Dave, and I'll be getting enough money for you to quit this work and finish your education. Now, tell Mr. Williams tomorrow that you want to quit."

I wanted to ask Aunt Mae a lot of things, but I didn't. I wanted to know what I was going to eat, and Mother too, with her gone off. And in Nashville with Clyde. I knew Clyde was old, but then I didn't know about him either. When I saw him with her, he didn't act old, and that was all else I knew. Quitting the job with Mr. Williams was something I didn't want to do. If I went and quit, I lost just about the best job I could get anywhere. And Mr. Williams would think I didn't appreciate what he did for me just giving me the job.

Aunt Mae passed by my chair and kissed me on top of my head. I didn't do anything but just kept looking out the back door to where Mother was somewhere in the pines. It was beginning to get dark, and she usually came in then. Pretty soon I saw her coming under the light green needles in the dimness with her skirt held up like a basket to hold some cones she must have picked up under the trees. I looked at her nearing the back steps and tried to think of living alone with her, even if it was for just two weeks. That funny tingling ran up the inside of my legs from my heels, and I just sat there and kept rubbing my finger over the worn-off places on the oilcloth.

Aunt Mae reached up and turned on the light when Mother came in. She went and closed the old screen because Mother's hands were holding in the cones. Mother came over to the table and dumped the cones out in a pile in the middle of the oilcloth. Her hands were all full of clay from pulling the cones out the ground, and leaves were stuck all in her skirt.

"There," she said.

I looked up at her, and she looked at me and smiled. I smiled back, but I was surprised at the way she looked. She looked like she got older during the day, even from when I saw her in the morning. I knew she was still looking at me, so I looked out the back door at the dark setting in between the pines, but I was thinking about how Mother looked with her face all like leather the way they stretched it to make drums, and her hair like white wire. I thought about her eyes with that funny look, and then I thought of when she was pretty and soft and I used to kiss her and hold on to her, but now I was afraid of her and didn't want to get near her.

Aunt Mae made a sign to me to leave the kitchen so Mother could eat.

The next day I went down to the store and told Mr. Williams I had to quit. He thought I was trying to make fun at first. Then I told him I really meant it, that I had to because Aunt Mae was leaving me with Mother for a while. He looked at me with that sad kind of look like Aunt Mae's, and I wished he would stop and let me go. He went over to the cash register and got out some money and put it in an envelope and gave it to me. I didn't know what to say, and I guess he didn't know either, so I left, but I did thank him, and I was glad. Then, on my way back up the hill, I thought maybe it was wrong to take the money from him. But I didn't go back.

The day after that was the day Aunt Mae was leaving. She didn't have enough money to take the train, so she was going on the bus. I watched her pack up in her room and helped her close the top of the old suitcase she owned. I was careful not to bend her scrapbook, which was right on top of her clothes, when I finally got the lock to snap. She put on her hat, the same one she wore the day she came to live with us, and she didn't even think about it, but I did.

When she was ready to leave, we looked for Mother, but

she wasn't anywhere around. I guessed she was in the back, but we didn't have time to find her. The bus came through in thirty minutes.

I picked up Aunt Mae's suitcase and looked at the stickers from New Orleans and Biloxi and Mobile while she got the hatpin through her hair. The wind was getting cold as we got on the porch, so I closed the front door behind us. As we walked down the path, Aunt Mae talked about what I was to do about food, and where to find the cans in the kitchen and the pan to fry eggs, and when she would write about the tickets, but I didn't listen to everything she said. I was thinking about the way we used to walk together when I was a little boy. Aunt Mae wore the same big hat then, but it looked a lot newer and brighter, and I never saw many big hats like that anymore. But Aunt Mae looked about the same, except she had clothes like anybody in the valley now, and not the different things she wore at first. It was when I was thinking that that I thought of how old Aunt Mae really was. I guess I never thought much about her age because she was so healthy the way she did everything. But Aunt Mae was really old, I thought all of a sudden, and I looked down at her hair. It was as yellow as always. And I felt sorry for her. I don't know why I did. Maybe it was thinking about her having to go all the way to Nashville and being with Clyde.

Fall was really all over the hills. The pines lashed each other in the wind up high, but down near the ground it was sort of still, and yet it was windy too, but not as windy as up high where the pines ended. Some leaves from the bushes that grew in the open blew around our feet and ran down the path in front of us to town. I wished I had a coat with me because my arms were beginning to get bumpy like they always did when it was cold. Aunt Mae didn't have a coat either, and I knew it was going to be even colder in Nashville, but when I told her she said we didn't have time to go back to the house to get one.

We got down into town under the bright blue sky. The leaves that had followed us down the hill joined some others in the streets and blew along in the gutters and up through yards and onto the windows of moving cars, where they stayed just like they were pasted until the car stopped moving. The bus stopped in front of the barbershop, so we got down to where it was on Main and waited by the curb. Aunt Mae's suitcase was heavy, and I was glad to put it down.

Aunt Mae looked down the street to see if the bus was coming, and when she turned around, I saw her eyes were wet along the bottom.

"It's the cold breeze, hon. Always makes my eyes water."

We waited there for what seemed a whole hour before the bus came. Then I heard it roaring somewhere far away, and I went out into the street to make a sign at the driver when he got near. It stopped about a block away. I picked up the suitcase, and we both ran to where the driver was opening the door. Aunt Mae got up on the first step and then got down again and kissed me, and I kissed her. I wanted to tell her not to go, but I handed her the suitcase, and the door closed. Somewhere in the dark inside I saw her waving at me. I waved back and smiled. Then the engine started and it pulled away. The bad smell of a bus got in my nose, so I stepped back on the sidewalk and watched it till it was gone around the far hill, and that was the last time I saw Aunt Mae.

# Nine

It was getting dark when I got back to the house. All the way up the path I thought of how long it would be until I got the tickets from Aunt Mae and what we would do until they came. The wind was really up strong now. It was cold too, and when I got near the house I began to run. I closed my eyes because I knew the path by heart and didn't open them again until I felt the cinders crunching under my feet.

When I got into the house I closed all the windows because the wind was blowing through every room like it was the outdoors. I lit the old stove in the kitchen and opened a can of corn and put it in a pot. Then I wondered where Mother was. I opened the back door and called out into the wind, but then I remembered she never answered a call from somebody, and anyway, she always came inside when it was dark. The dark scared her.

149

She was probably upstairs, so I didn't think about it. When the corn was hot, I poured it in a plate and put some butter on it and got some bread and ate. The wind whistled around the corner of the kitchen, and I heard the pines in Poppa's clearing slapping each other with that sort of swishing sound they made. I could see the hill in the morning with needles and small branches everywhere and leaves from the bushes pressed up against everything. The cinders would be all covered with green things from all over, and the little animals would be acting wild. The wind always made them that way.

When I finished, I put the plate in the sink with all the other dishes. I looked at all the greasy plates and glasses, and I thought of how I was going to have to wash them all and wished Aunt Mae didn't take too long to write about the tickets. Then I stood there and thought how she just went off and didn't think about me taking Mother on a train, and I thought of leaving the valley. I was going to leave the valley for the first time, but Aunt Mae never told me anything about what to do about the things we had in the house, and there were a lot of other things you had to do before you could just pick up and move, and I didn't know where to write her a letter about what I was supposed to do. I looked up at the old greasy bulb on the cord. It never seemed to burn out, but it was the one we used all the time. I never remembered seeing anybody change it. And I thought that I was really alone with Mother like that bulb hanging from a cord it couldn't get off of.

As I went into the hall, the wind pulled the front door open and slammed it again. I felt the cold breeze blow past me on its way back to the kitchen. I had put a little latch on the door to lock it at night because there were a few more people around in the hills with all the new houses, and I went over and tried to hook it, but a screw was loose or something and it wouldn't work, so I just hoped the wind didn't get in again.

The stairs were all worn so that you had to put your feet where everybody else put theirs when they went up. Every step had two spots, both along the side, where the wood was about an inch lower than it was in the middle and at the end of the steps. Sometimes to be different I'd walk right up the center of the steps where nobody ever did. I did that now. I walked right in the middle where the wood looked like it was new. There were sixteen steps up to the top floor. I counted them as I walked up. Thirteen. Fourteen. I wondered what I was going to do around the house waiting for a letter from Aunt Mae. There wasn't anybody to talk to, and I never had read books like Mr. Farney said people should learn to so they could make themselves smarter and have something good for when they were lonely and didn't know what to do with themselves. Fifteen. There was something wet on the step right in a puddle in one of the worn places on the side. In the dark I couldn't see too well, but there was a little light from down in the kitchen, and I could see it wasn't water. It was too thick and dark. There was some more on the top step too, so I put my hand in it and rubbed it between my fingers, but I didn't know what it was. It looked sort of brown in the dimness.

I got to the top and started down the hall, but I stumbled over something that felt hard against my shoe. I stopped and tried to see what it was, but I couldn't make out any-thing in the dark, so I felt my way over to the lightbulb we had on the wall. When I pulled the cord and looked around, I saw something that I didn't think was real. Mother was

laying out in the hall with blood coming out her mouth. It
had flowed over to the steps because that was the way the
floor leaned, and that was what I had felt in my hand. I
looked at my hand. Blood was stuck in the cracks in my
fingers and was starting to get dry where it was thin. I wiped
my hands on my pants and went over to where she was. Just
looking at her made me scared. I thought she was dead, but
when I got down and touched her arm it was still warm, and
I could hear her breathing loud. The blood was getting all
stuck in her hair and was making a little shallow pool around
her. I put my hand over her mouth to try and stop more
from coming out, but when I took my hand away after a
while, all that I had been holding in poured out all at once
and made a little wave down the side of her face and neck
and made the border of the pool on the floor get wider.

My mind couldn't seem to tell me what to do. I thought I
felt my chin start to go in like it did when I was little, but I
knew I was too old to cry. What I had to do was to try to
think what I was supposed to do with her like that. Somewhere I had heard you shouldn't move people who were like
that, but I couldn't let her stay on the floor because it was
getting cold. I bent down near her face and began saying,
"Mother, Mother," but she didn't move, so I put my hands
under her, one by her back and one by her legs, and I carried
her into the room where she slept. Mother was so skinny and
her skin was so stretched-looking, but she was heavy, and
once I was worried I was going to drop her. All the way into
the room blood dripped from her dress and kept pouring
from her mouth. Her hair was hanging down, and it was all
white near her head, but it was red where it was in the pool
on the floor, and blood dripped off the ends of it too.

I put her on the bed and put an old blanket over her mouth so it would soak up the blood. After I did this, I sat down on the edge of the bed and looked at her. Her arm was right next to me, so I ran my hand along it and took her hand and held it. I wondered what was wrong. This was the first time I thought about it long enough to wonder. Blood coming out of her mouth. I rocked the bed a little bit and called her name, but she didn't answer. The wind just kept blowing around the house, and the front door slammed hard again and sounded far off.

Now I was afraid, and I didn't know what to do. Where could I get a doctor, and what would I pay him with? We needed the money I had in the house to eat. Doctors were expensive, especially for something like this that looked like it would cost a lot. We never did have a doctor up at the house, and I didn't know where to get one. I thought maybe if I kept Mother quiet, she would be better in the morning. The blood had stopped flowing, so that looked better, but it was all over the bed now, and it was starting to get sticky on the sheet. I went and got a wet rag and wiped her face and neck and got all the blood off that wasn't too stuck.

As I wiped around her mouth, I looked at her. This wasn't Mother, all brown and dried out and covered with sticky blood. I ran my hand on her forehead like I used to when it was white and soft, but it was dry and hard and dark. She was breathing hard, and sometimes it sounded something like a sigh, a sort of choking sigh. The bed looked too big for her, so small and dry in the light that came through the door from the hall, the dim yellow light that made her look even worse.

Then I was crying, and I didn't want to. I had to think of

what I was going to do with her here and Aunt Mae gone. My mother was dying. I knew it, and I couldn't do anything about it. The wind just blew cold and strong against the window in the room. It was the only other thing besides me and Mother up there on the hill. I held my hands up to my eyes like I was afraid somebody would see me and think I was too old to do it, and I cried like I never cried in my life, even when I was little. I couldn't stop, and I tried to catch my breath, but all of the things that had gone wrong came into my mind, and I put my head up against Mother on the bed and held her in my arms and cried on her hard chest like I did when it was full and round.

I felt her tremble. Something made me look up at her face, and her lips were moving. I tried to understand what she was saying, but they just moved for a while without making any sound, dry and cracked and with blood caked on them. The wind began blowing stronger and louder, so I got up closer to her face to hear, and she said, "Frank," and the breathing stopped, and she laid still in my arms.

All that night I stayed in the room where my train was. The wind howled and whistled and shook the house, and I was frightened. My mother was dead in the next room with a blanket over her. It was cold in the house, in the room where I was and in the next room too, but I guess it was colder in that room.

The night seemed like it would never get light again and like the wind would never stop. I sat down on the floor next to the rusty train and felt the wind blow in through the cracks in the wall and the openings around the window. My arms got full of little bumps, and I felt them on my legs too. I don't know why, but I kept thinking about Jo Lynne and the night in the new houses, and I wondered what she was doing now and where she was. But all the time I was still frightened and thinking about what I was going to do, too.

What would I do about burying Mother? I didn't know where I could write to Aunt Mae. She would tell me what to do, but I couldn't get her. And I thought about how much it cost to bury somebody. I didn't hardly have any money but what Mr. Williams gave me in the envelope, and that wouldn't do anything. If you didn't have the money to bury somebody, the state took care of them and buried them in some place in the capital without a name on the stone. Mother couldn't go there, and I couldn't wait a week to hear from Aunt Mae. You couldn't wait a week to bury somebody, either.

The light came up at last, first thin and pink, and then red and strong. I got up and went downstairs because I was hungry. There were some eggs in the kitchen, so I fried one and ate it, but I had let it in the pan too long, and it was brown on the bottom and tough. The yellow tasted creamy and good, but I had to chew the white a long time before it would break up and I could swallow it.

When the day was in full, I saw it was going to be an early winter day with a bright blue sky and a cold breeze blowing through the hills. The sun was out, so I put on my coat and went and sat on the back steps. I wanted to be out of the house so maybe I could think about what I was going to do, but my mind wouldn't settle on one thing. I thought about a whole lot of different things while I sat there, and I could only get one thing clear.

I got the shovel that Poppa bought when he started to

plant the clearing. It was under the house, all rusty, and had spider webs on the handle, so I wiped it off with a piece of paper before I used it. Back in the clearing I couldn't decide where to start digging. There were a lot of places that looked good. I finally picked a place between two pretty pines where it was dark and the wind was combed out until it was just a slight breeze. The clay was soft, so it was easy to dig. The only trouble I had was with roots, but there weren't too many of them, and they broke off pretty clean when I hit them with the shovel blade. The breeze blew some needles and cones down into the hole, and some bush leaves. And it blew more things up against the pile of clay that was building up where I shoveled it. I hit some rocks too, but they weren't big ones, just little gray chips.

By the time I finished it was getting warmer, but the breeze was still up through the pines. I could see by the sun that it was just about noon. There weren't any shadows in the hole now except for the ones the pine branches above made, and the trunks didn't have any dark twin hanging behind them. The morning was over. I felt hungry again, so I went in the house and found another can in the kitchen. It was just tomatoes. I ate them out the can without heating them, and they needed salt.

It was colder in the house than it was outside. I had left the windows closed, and the cold air from the night was still all over everything. I would go upstairs in a little while, I thought, and get her, but I'd rather just sit in the kitchen now a while. Just as I was finishing a glass of water, I heard something moving around on the front porch, and the door opened. Aunt Mae kept Poppa's old gun in the kitchen in case somebody or some animal came around when she was there with Mother. I never knew why, because they didn't have any big enough animals in the hills and no people ever came up near the house, but I took the gun from behind the stove now, although I never had used one in my life.

By the footsteps in the hall I knew it was a man. Then he coughed and broke the still and cold of the house. I got the gun and put it by the kitchen door and went into the hall.

"Hello there, Robert."

It was the preacher.

"My name's David." I wondered what he was doing in the house.

"David. Pardon me. It's just so long since I've known your family at the church."

I didn't say anything, and when he saw I wasn't going to talk, he went on again.

"Well, I see your aunt has gone away, son, and I might as well get down to brass tacks, as the expression goes. I'm here on behalf of the state, son. Now, you know your mother needs a better place to stay, and you can't take care of her here by yourself. When your aunt was here it was different, but now with her gone . . ."

"What do you want?" I kept my eyes on him, but he was looking all over the place and never looked at me.

"Now, I have my car at the bottom of the hill, and I'm ready to take her off to a very nice place not far from here. You know where I'm talking about. She'll be happy there, son. This is no place for her to be with just a boy and all. Get a few of her clean dresses together, if you will. Now, is she upstairs? Go get her down here. I'll just sit in the front room and wait."

"She isn't going with you. She isn't here," I said as he started to walk to the old couch. He turned around.

"Now, son, maybe you don't understand. It's for your own good, and for the town too. As a Christian, I want to see that what's done is the best for all. I'll go up and get her myself."

He walked over to the stairs and started up, but I called to him.

"She's not up there. Anyway, you can't come in here like that. Get out of here. You hear me, get out of here. Get off those steps, damn you, before I come pull you off and get the sheriff. Get the hell out of this house, you bastard, I know what you . . ."

"I won't listen to any more of your profanity, boy. Keep your peace and be grateful that someone has enough interest to work for you and help you in the name of the Lord!"

He started up the steps again, and I ran back in the kitchen and got the gun. I aimed and fired just as he got to the top. The gun kicked me up against the wall, and when I got my balance again, I saw him falling forward. He didn't scream or anything like I had expected from the movies. He just fell there at the top of the steps and laid quiet.

I dropped the gun and stared up at the top of the steps. He didn't move. He was sprawled out with his head and hands in the hall upstairs and his body down on the steps. The back of his head was beginning to get red, a bright sort of red.

When I got up enough courage to look at it, I walked up the steps to where he was. I had shot him through the back of the head right near where his neck began. The blood pumped out in little spurts and flowed from the hall onto the top step, where it made a new pool in one of the worn-out foot spots over Mother's blood that was caked from the night before. I stayed up against the rail on the other side of the steps and didn't get near him, and I didn't know if he was alive or dead. When the blood didn't stop, I turned my head away and looked down in the hall near the kitchen where the gun was on the floor. Then I looked back at him. The blood had stopped, and I felt sick in the stomach. I had killed somebody.

The cold in the house made me shiver even though I had a coat on. I ran down the upstairs hall and went into the room where the train was and slammed the door. I tried to open the window to let some of the warm outside air in, but it wouldn't move. My legs were tingling up and down the inside, and I felt it grab me right up between them. Outside the pines were blowing in the breeze. The sun was all over everything, and the sky was that bright clear blue that hurts your eyes if you look at it. But it was cold and dark in the house, and I wanted to get outside in the warmth and sun. I had to do something first, though.

It was cold and darker, I thought, in the room where Mother was. Under the cover I could see her shape, but not too well. The only parts that stuck up were her feet and head. The rest was sunken in and looked like just part of the mattress, but I knew she was there, and it made me scared. Without taking the old blanket off, I put my hands under her and picked her up. She was heavier than I thought she would be, and her cold and stiffness made me want to put her down and wash my hands and get out of the house.

As I carried her past where the preacher was, the blanket dragged through the blood and made a trail down the steps until I got to the kitchen door, where it stopped leaving a red trail but just made the floor damp. I had to put Mother down to open the back door, and the blanket fell away from her legs, and I saw them stiff and cold and brown. Before I picked her up again, I threw the blanket back in place so I wouldn't see any of her. The hard brown flesh made my stomach turn over.

When I had filled in the hole back in the clearing, I threw leaves and needles and scattered things over it so nobody would know where it was and disturb it. Then I saw that the mound still showed, so I got the shovel and leveled it off and threw the dirt all over. Then I put some more branches and things over it, and I thought it looked the best I could make it.

I went and threw the shovel way under the house and was going off, but I went back to the clearing and got down on my knees where the things were all scattered, and I prayed, and the pines began to make longer shadows over the place. Then I knew I couldn't stay any longer.

The envelope Mr. Williams gave me was in my coat pocket, so I went out of the clearing and looked back once and went on down the path. I walked through town and said hello to people I knew, but I didn't look back at our hill or the house or what was in it. Nobody had heard the shot. The house was too far away from anything else, and they always had hunters up in the hills.

The man at the train stop said there was one coming in in about half an hour, but he didn't know where it was going. I sat down on the bench there and waited.

# Ten

So here I am on the train. Dawn is coming up. I can see it through the windows on the other side of the car, pink and a little yellow at the top and dark red at the bottom. The car is almost empty, except for me and an old woman up front and a soldier across from me. All night we stopped and people got off.

By now I can't say how far away from the valley I am, but it must be quite a way. I've been riding since before the night first came on, and we've been going pretty fast, though not as fast as we could, because this looks like an old train. At least the seats are old and uncomfortable, and I never did go to sleep.

This is flat country. No hills to talk about now that I can see it. I never been in flat country, and I wonder what it's like to live around here. I'm used to hills, I guess, and pines, but

161

they don't have any trees like that around here, just low flat-looking ones that look like they wouldn't move in any kind of breeze.

I didn't ask the conductor where this train went. I know I should, but I just gave him Mr. Williams' envelope and told him to let me off where it didn't pay for the ride anymore. He hasn't come by yet, though he's passed down the aisle a couple of times lately, and I thought he was coming to see me and tap me on the shoulder, but he hasn't, so I guess I have a while more to go. I hope I get off in a city, a big one. I always wanted to see a city, and you can get jobs there, and people don't ask a lot of questions like they do in a place like the valley.

Maybe they're up at the house now, too. The preacher's wife would get somebody to go see where he was, I guess, but I'm not so scared now with the train getting this far away.

I want to write a letter to Aunt Mae. When I find out where I am and get a job, maybe I'll save some money and go to Nashville and look for her. I guess they think that's where I am, that I went to look for her.

The sun's up full now over the short trees, and I can see the sky's the same clear blue that it was yesterday in the valley.